From Whom No Secrets are Hidden

The first Adam Pennycome novel

From Whom No Secrets are Hidden

The first Adam Pennycome novel

Tim Buckley

Dedication

To Kaz who encouraged me to keep on writing.

A b o u t   t h e   A u t h o r

Revd Tim Buckley is a vicar, novelist and poet striving to tell a better story. His first novel, the Drumchester Diaries, was published in March 2022 to critical acclaim. He can be contacted via his website: *revtim.uk*

Almighty God, to whom all hearts are open, all desires known,
and from whom no secrets are hidden...
(The Anglican Prayer of Preparation)

Chapter 1

THE COLD NOVEMBER DELUGE HIT Adam in the face as soon as he came out of the courtroom. Usually he would have checked the weather forecast well in advance and taken appropriate measures. But today he hadn't and today he didn't mind. He stood quite still for a moment, feeling the rain soak through his hair, then his jacket, and then down his back, as if ritually cleansing himself from the first day of the trial.

Adam had always accepted it was part of his job to attend court and in the normal course of events it was a task he undertook with reasonable equilibrium. But this trial was different for all kinds of reasons, and Adam knew just how much he was personally invested in the outcome.

The accused had sat quite still behind the Perspex screen all day, with barely a flicker of emotion, not even when the mother of the victim broke down while the evidence was presented in full forensic detail. He remained steadfastly unmoved, his head slightly bowed, his keen blue eyes focused resolutely on some point a little way ahead of him. Only at the very end of the proceedings did he turn and face Adam directly, as if issuing some kind of challenge. Was that a smirk behind his face mask? Or a sardonic smile? It was hard to tell. All Adam knew was that the old man in him wanted to rip that mask off and punch him hard, while the new man whispered something about the fruit of the Spirit being self-control.

Conscious of how wet and cold he was, Adam found shelter in a nearby coffee shop. Later he would go out to his sister Sally in Harold Hill, but right at this moment the bustle of a chaotic family life was the last thing he needed. He ordered a double shot espresso and checked his messages. He ignored nearly every one of them until he found the one he wanted to read, from his fiancée Sadie. They had planned to marry back in June, but coronavirus had disrupted their plans, as for so many others, and Adam missed her terribly. Still, he had spent much of the last few years waiting for her and he reasoned that sooner or later the waiting had to be over.

So, taking a sip of his espresso, and checking he really was on his own, Adam clicked on her email and began to read:

How did today go? I have been thinking of you and praying so much today. I am very aware you can't share any details, but I hope you always know you are in my heart. I have some good news, yesterday I managed to walk to the cornershop without stopping on the way. And today I actually managed an hour on the computer without the usual brain fog. So slowly I am recovering, and I fully intend to come to you as soon as this trial is over. How soon can we get married? I am determined nothing stops us this time!

P.S. I noticed this article on the London news, I thought you might be interested.

Adam smiled as he absorbed her words. After a hard, cruel summer it was good to see Sadie getting some of her drive back, and the prospect of a wedding would at least provide some measure of distraction during this awful trial. He would ring later that evening, but they had already long agreed that if restrictions meant only they and a few others could be there, they would still tie the knot.

Adam had finished his cup, before he remembered the attachment. It was a very prosaic article about a long overdue redevelopment. Yet when he read it, he found himself laughing out loud – not because the words were funny, but because once again those three strands of his life were interweaving. Somewhere, he felt, the Lord was showing once again a grim sense of humour.

~ * ~ * ~ * ~

Magnolia House was an unloved and unwanted example of Brutalist architecture in a forgotten and unregenerate corner of London. Up until the point of construction it had been a Socialist utopia, the last in a series of tower blocks named after flowers that never had a hope of growing in their unforgiving concrete aprons. It was wedged tightly in the armpit of a railway intersection where overground and tube trains rattled past indifferently day and night.

As a young constable, DS Adam Pennycome had visited the estate several times and on every occasion come away with a feeling of deep, deep depression. Today was a beautiful summer day with a clear azure sky but the heat reflecting off the forecourt and the stench of uncollected rubbish only created a heavy, foetid atmosphere.

Adam noticed the CCTV over the entrance was broken. Inside someone had tried their hardest to paint over the graffiti but no amount of decorating could disguise the aroma of urine and cannabis that lingered in the stairwell. There was no ventilation; a heavy grille had been placed over the window and by the time Adam reached the fifth floor, he was already sweating and secretly hoping his visit would be mercifully brief.

Alas, it was not to be. He was greeted by the crime scene officer, a jovial Scot called Jennie, who introduced him to the deceased. Niall

O'connor sat in a threadbare chair, his body already rigid, the lips in his gaunt, pale face tinged with blue. There was a syringe next to him, and the only real wonder was how he had found a vein. He wore a dirty blue vest that exposed all the sites where he had injected himself over the years, and the bare floor was littered with every manner of drug paraphernalia.

"It seems a fairly routine OD," said Adam, trying hard not to step on anything that might be evidence, "but I am guessing there's a good reason why I am here."

"Follow me," said Jennie with a smile. She led him into the bedroom which was almost empty apart from a chest of drawers, a hanger with a few worn out clothes on it and a bed covered in foul smelling blankets that obviously had not been washed in a while.

"So," explained Jennie, "we were doing a concern for welfare check. PC McQueen found the deceased, realised there was nothing she could do, and called it in. But before she left, she had a good look round and under the bed she found these."

Jennie lifted up the dirty blankets and with her gloved hands pulled out two suitcases, one containing carefully wrapped bags of heroin, the other equally well wrapped bags of cash.

"She's a good copper that's for sure," said Adam, who admitted he was not completely impartial on the subject. "I think we can rule out the deceased being a major dealer, can't we?"

"Apparently so," said Jennie. They paused for a moment to survey the scene. The clothes on the hanger were faded and worn, the furniture probably the offcasts of some local charity shop. The only personal item was a framed photo of the deceased, taken at some point in his childhood, wearing a Newcastle United shirt. There was a slightly older girl standing next to him, oddly watchful and wary, with a protective arm thrown round his shoulder.

"Could that be a sister?"

"Could well be," said Jennie. "She is the one who raised the alarm. Only recently got back in touch with her brother, used to ring every day. She sensed he was scared of something, but she said he didn't seem free to talk."

"Where is she now?"

"Coming down from Newcastle as soon as she can. The coach gets in sometime late this evening."

Adam nodded. "You know what to do here, I will start work outside. Just one question – have you found any phones?"

"That's the odd thing," replied Jennie, "so far the team haven't found anything…"

"…which at least suggests some kind of interference in the crime scene. OK, Jennie, let's catch up later."

As Adam left the flat, the team were starting to load the drugs and cash into evidence bags. He went out through the back door and was once again hit by the stifling heat reflecting off the surface of the hard, unforgiving courtyard. Halfway across, there was a solitary children's pink bicycle abandoned beneath a line of washing, lending an air of sadness to the scene. He made his way to the bin store where torn black sacks were overflowing from the bins. He wondered which poor sod would end up sorting out that lot. In the meanwhile he rang Jennie to make sure the rubbish dump was secured.

He walked up the broken steps across the service lane to Lilac House. He noted that the CCTV there seemed to be working. That, at least, was something. He rang DI Spencer to arrange a team to conduct door to door enquiries, and review CCTV. He highly doubted very much of use would turn up, but he would, as always, do the job as professionally as possible.

The coach from Newcastle broke down on the way, and by the time

Maire arrived, it was too late to interview her. As expected, almost no-one in the flats had answered to the knock of a passing detective, and those who responded were all in need of an interpreter. Adam knew it was still very early in the investigation but even so, the apparent futility of his efforts so far made him long for the cricket practice he was missing. He flighted a scrunched up piece of paper but his legbreak missed the bin. It was already almost midnight. Adam sighed and knew it was time to go home.

It was nearly one o'clock by the time Adam reached his flat just south of the river. He had missed the last tube train, and it was a hot, humid walk home under a heavy yellow moon. By the time he reached his front door, he realised he hadn't eaten properly since lunchtime, and he was in desperate need of nutrition.

He almost tripped over the large manilla envelope on his doormat. Puzzled, Adam picked it up and placed it on the lounge table. It was from a firm of solicitors in Devon, marked "urgent". Wondering what to do about it, Adam put some pasta on to boil, and then checked his personal emails. There was a message from his younger sister Jo talking about her noisy neighbours and the problem with her landlord. And one from Sadie asking if they could meet up soon. Adam smiled faintly. He never quite knew when Sadie would next come into his life, only that sooner or later they would always pick up where they had left off, as if their conversation had never really ended.

As he mentally composed a reply, the timer went off. Adam drained the pasta, added some tomato sauce, cheese and a tin of tuna. He had never believed in living off junk food, and secretly dreamed of one day having his own allotment, just like his grandad had back in the day. But for now his life was in the Thameside Serious Crimes' Unit or "Tescu's" as it was not so affectionately known.

Instinctively Adam settled down in front of the TV. He had planned to leave the envelope until morning when his head was clearer. But something kept nagging at him to open it. He had only received letters like this at the station before and he was very careful never to reveal his home address. Carefully he unstuck the flap, as if there might be something poisonous inside. But the only contents were a plain, headed sheet of notepaper.

Dear Mr Pennycome,

I regret to inform you that your great-uncle David Arthur Pennycome passed away two days ago at Shortsands Nursing Home. He listed you as next of kin but as I only had your correspondence address have unfortunately been compelled to write to you. Please can you telephone my number as soon as you receive this letter to discuss registering the death and arrangements for the funeral.

Your uncle David often spoke warmly of you and as the executor of his estate I am also writing to inform you that you are the sole beneficiary of his will. I am sure you will in due course wish to visit my offices and discuss the property that has been settled on you.

Yours faithfully,

Christopher Brunt, Solicitor

Adam read and reread the letter several times. His great uncle David had always been full of surprises, but this was the greatest surprise of all.

He had last visited his uncle about six months ago. David was sitting in a chair, frail and thin, with gravy stains streaking his threadbare jumper. Looking back Adam would have liked to say he was visiting out of family duty. But in reality he needed to use his annual leave. His parents were settling into semi-retirement in Spain. His older sister Sally was up to her ears with her three children, and Jo's flat was too tiny for visitors. So he spent a week in the far South West of England, spending the days tracking down his distant ancestors, and the evenings working out in a local gym.

David's nursing home lay on the way back in the gentle countryside of an East Devon valley. It had been a while since Adam had seen his uncle and he was shocked by his physical decline. Yet for all his frailty, David's mind was as sharp as ever. He told stories of his time in the force, when poverty was greater but drugs largely unknown and abuse almost never mentioned. And he talked about his time after the force, when, pensioned out because of a back injury, he had travelled throughout Europe selling office equipment, often in the most unlikely of places. After about half an hour these stories became more muddled, and Adam couldn't be sure which phase of his life David was talking about. Soon it was time for David to take his pills, and Adam quickly swallowed the dregs of his thin, lukewarm tea. But as he made to go, David firmly grasped him by his hand and said, "You're a good lad. Keep catching the bastards." And for some reason Adam then kissed him on the forehead.

Adam must have dozed after reading the letter. It was after five when he woke, his head full of vague memories he hadn't quite captured in his dreams. He made a pot of strong coffee and then went for a run. The early morning sun was already beating down to warm the stale city air, so today wasn't going to be his best time. But that didn't really matter. He needed to clear his head, and be ready for whatever the coming day would bring.

The station where Adam worked looked as if it had been made out of corrugated cardboard sometime in the 1970s. It was freezing cold in winter and now, in the middle of summer, blazing hot, and the flimsy blinds were no match for the sunshine blazing through the thin metal framed windows. Adam was impatient to see DI Spencer but some minor drama at home meant he was late in.

So in the meanwhile Adam interviewed Niall's sister Maire. She had the same spare, gaunt figure as her brother, and Adam noticed one of the tattoos on her right arm bore his initials. She sat still, impassive as if this was an event she had been expecting for a long time. "I always knew the heroin would kill him one day," she said in her thick Geordie accent, without any obvious trace of emotion.

"How long had he been using?"

"He started when he was 15, so, yeah, about 25 years."

"And what took him to London?"

"He thought he could start a new life. I told him London was going to be nae different, but he didna want to listen."

"And you only recently got back in touch?"

Maire smiled for the first time, and Adam could see that beneath the tired, careworn exterior there once had been a bright, intelligent young woman. "For some reason he didna send me his address. And life was tough for me as well," she continued more seriously, "but once I was able to start looking, I wasn't going to stop until I found him."

"How did he react when you got in touch?"

"Relieved, I think. I was shocked how ill he sounded, but I was glad at least he was alive."

"And why did you make a concern for welfare call?"

"'Cos I know my wee brother and right from that first phone call he sounded scared. Shit-scared. As if he wasn't free to speak his mind, as if someone else was controlling him or using him."

Adam thought for a moment. He had come across more and more cases of cuckooing recently, and all the evidence suggested Niall did not even have the safety of his own home. Whoever was behind his death needed to be caught, even if they weren't directly responsible for his death.

"So what happened the last time you tried to ring him?"

"I tried to get through three or four times. Every time before he had answered in the end, or got back to me as soon as he could. But not this time. I waited five, ten, thirty minutes, and I knew something was wrong. Don't ask me how I knew. I knew," she said firmly, fixing Adam with her gaze.

"Just one more question," added Adam, "did Niall ever lose his phone?"

Maire looked at him quizzically. "No," said Maire slowly, "his phone was his lifeline. Why do you ask?"

Adam shook his head. "I'm afraid I can't give you any further details."

Maire smiled again, but this time only to let Adam know she knew the rules of the game. Adam made a mental note to check her record and then invited her to identify her brother.

By now DI Spencer had arrived in his office. He was a tall, balding figure who told everyone he believed in being firm but fair. He was also an avid supporter of Brentford FC and a signed team photo above the desk was the only personal touch in this cramped, airless space that always reeked of sweat, and takeaways consumed in the most antisocial hours of the night. Adam reported the progress, or lack of it, in the case so far then told DI Spencer about the mysterious letter he had found on his doormat.

"Not the best time for it to turn up, is it?" said DI Spencer, stirring sugar into a chipped mug of builder's tea, "but then, death has a habit of being inconvenient, doesn't it?" He took a slurp, added more sugar and then said, "Well, it sounds like we're not going to get very far until forensics come in. That's likely to be Monday, so why don't you take a long weekend off this Friday?"

Adam grimaced. He hated taking time off during a case. But he couldn't really see an alternative, and besides, he had to use up his leave somehow. So with some reluctance he made a phone call, and then got back to the task in hand. If nothing else, he felt he owed Maire, and the one thing he wanted was never to be in anyone's debt.

Chapter 2

WITH SOME RELUCTANCE ADAM BOARDED a train to Exeter that Friday. He found a seat in the quiet carriage, took his phone and appeared to be playing some kind of game. In reality he mentally reviewed progress on the case so far and put the various leads into some kind of order. So, first of all, the door to door interviews. Despite the apparent futility of the effort, he had, as usual, doggedly persisted. However, the few who made a response all claimed complete ignorance of any activity in Niall's flat. Yes, they had seen the deceased a few times, but, no, they had never been aware of any visitors. Niall was a quiet tenant who kept himself to himself, and that was the line everyone repeated in whatever language they happened to speak. He had tried to press one or two further, but the sudden look of fear in their eyes told him all he needed to know. Niall's flat was a cuckoo's nest, and he just needed now to find the evidence.

His colleague, DS Emma Sutton, had spoken to the housing association but the officer who had the delightful duty of managing Magnolia House had gone off sick. She was going to follow that lead up today. Adam hoped against hope she would tell him the results of her investigation, but he doubted that she would. Emma was ambitious, and knowledge in a case represented power. He sighed, and realised he would simply have to wait for Monday, almost no matter what happened.

The catch up with SCO Jennie was altogether more straightforward, if equally unrewarding. Despite a fingertip search, no sign of a phone or card had been found, and the bin had been emptied as well. As for the garbage in the courtyard, it was so mixed up with waste from all the other flats it was almost impossible to secure any meaningful evidence.

The only additional information had come from the interview with PC Blessing McQueen. Blessing was a tall, elegant woman, originally from Zimbabwe, with long, smooth limbs, and perfectly white teeth. Adam had dated her a couple of times, and would probably have slept with her, if it wasn't for Sadie. But he had decided to keep the relationship professional, and they had ever since kept an appropriate distance.

So with her on one side of the desk, and him on the other, Blessing related her discovery of the body. The call about Niall had come in the night before, but the whole station had been slammed, and it was left to her to follow up when she came on shift. She turned up at Magnolia House at 8.15am. The front door was, as Adam expected, locked, so like everyone else she went round the back. Did she notice anyone else around? There was a mother and her young daughter heading out somewhere, but otherwise there were few signs of life. Only she couldn't be sure, but she felt someone watching her from Lilac House. How did she know? There was a curtain twitching on the second floor, but she guessed it could have been the breeze, she didn't actually see anyone.

So what did you do when you arrived at the flat? She had knocked and then waited, and then knocked again. When there was no reply, she phoned the housing association, and waited for someone to bring the key. It took about half an hour for a lady called Chloe to turn up. She had entered alone, and that is when she came across the late Mr

O'connor. She asked Chloe to wait outside while she rang the station then she proceeded to look round the flat. And why did she do that? She'd heard one or two rumours – nothing more than that – about Magnolia House and drugs, and thought she ought to check. Had she seen any phones? No, of that she was sure. She told CID of her discovery, then waited outside until Jennie and the team turned up. Did she see anyone during that time? Yes, Niall's neighbour came out briefly but retreated when he saw the uniform.

The train was pulling into Taunton at this point. Adam knew this neighbour, as one of the many who had refused to answer any questions. He had concluded the interview at this point, and watched as Blessing gracefully exited the room. Every time he saw or thought of Blessing, he found himself reviewing his decision to stick with Sadie. He was sure a relationship with Blessing would have brought a great deal of pleasure to both of them. And yet...

Adam and Sadie had met in their second year at university. It was a fresh spring day, and Adam had gone down early to men's outdoor nets because he was hoping to see a girl he fancied while the women were still practising. As it turned out she wasn't there, and Adam barely saw her again.

Sadie was sitting on a bank nursing a bang on her hand. A delivery had reared up unexpectedly and she had applied an icepack to the bruise. She was not best pleased when Adam wandered over to her.

"That looks sore," said Adam.

"Do you use that chat-up line with every girl you meet?" replied Sadie crossly. Then she said, "Sorry, that wasn't very polite of me."

"Say a stupid statement, get a stupid answer," said Adam and despite her pain Sadie laughed.

"OK, let's try again. I'm Sadie Quick but despite my name I never bowl. And you, I think you must be Adam Pennycome... OK, I've stopped to see the men practise a few times. And there's definitely only one person in the squad who's trying to bowl like Shane Warne..."

"...And failing miserably. Although let's get the jokes out of the way, my googly is improving."

"I wasn't laughing," said Sadie, looking up at him. Adam saw a rather plain girl with tousled, auburn hair, and strikingly green eyes, definitely not his type at all. Sadie, as she told him many years later, saw a rather over-confident boy with a crew cut and fierce dark eyes, set in an angular, square-cut face.

"So what are you studying?" she asked. When Adam told her politics, she was surprised. "You don't look like a politics student."

"And what does a politics student look like?"

"Depends. If he's a conservative, he has a posh accent and wears a tweed jacket and corduroys. If he's a socialist, he tries to sound common, and wears a donkey jacket or parka. But you're neither. Let me guess... you're studying politics because you had a teacher at school that inspired you, and now you are rather regretting your choice."

"That's impressive," said Adam and for the first time they looked directly at each other. "So what about you?"

"Oh, I'm studying business and finance," replied Sadie.

"You don't exactly sound happy about it."

"It's only because my parents own a hotel, and they want someone to run it after they retire. I keep hoping my older brother Kevin will take it on, but at the moment he's quite sensibly backpacking through South America, keeping as far away from the hotel as possible."

Adam wanted to carry on the conversation, but a couple of Sadie's friends came over to find out how she was doing, and Adam felt awkward standing there. So he went down to the nets and started turning over his arm. But he knew he and Sadie would meet again and soon. What he could not foresee, of course, was how their friendship would develop into an enduring relationship which somehow still survived, despite the years of separation.

The train was arriving now at Exeter St David's. Adam realised he hadn't yet replied to Sadie's message. But a delay of a few days was not that critical, and besides, there would be plenty more to tell once this strange meeting was over.

So Adam picked up a hire car and headed out east to a small market town called Heronford. As he drove along the broad high street full of antique shops and eateries of every kind, Adam noticed how quiet the place seemed, even in high season. His Satnav took him right at the end of the street past some anonymous housing estates that could have belonged in any town. The registry office, when he found it, was depressingly similar to his own police station, a stack of concrete shoeboxes with the same thin metal-framed windows that no doubt also leaked, and the same set of steps chipped and faded that led to a heavy, unwelcoming front door.

"Depressing, isn't it?" said a polished, bass voice behind him. "And yet some people choose to get married here."

"DS Adam Pennycome."

"DS, eh? Might mean there is at least one honest client in the world." Christopher Brunt was exactly as Adam imagined him from his voice on the phone: grey-haired, upright, with gold-rimmed spectacles and a finely tailored suit. They went into the stuffy reception area where calmly and efficiently Christopher went through all the paperwork.

Half an hour later they were standing outside, glad of a soft, late afternoon breeze that cooled the shadow of the grim edifice. "Where are you staying tonight?"

"I booked a room at the Crown and Cushion."

"Comfortable," said the solicitor, smiling, "even if the food is stuck in the 1970s." Then he hesitated for a moment. "Do you fancy seeing the house?"

"What house?" asked Adam blankly.

"The house which, if no-one contests the will, is now yours."

It took a moment for Adam to take in what he was saying. He had always met his uncle at pubs or on family holidays, and he had never really thought where David lived. "Of course, we could wait until we have finished the paperwork on Monday," Christopher continued, "it might be the wiser course of action."

Soon Adam was being driven out of town up a steep hill. He found himself in broken countryside dotted with straggling villages and small, neat churches through which the road twisted and turned. Eventually, as the road veered steeply right, Christopher turned left down a narrow lane which plunged through thick woodland down to an ancient stone bridge. They crossed the river and the road climbed briefly before turning left through open parkland. On the bend was a driveway leading up an avenue of lime trees. To the left of this avenue stood a lodge surrounded by high, overgrown laurels with a scrubby copse behind. Christopher swung his Saab through the gap in the hedge. "Hope I still have the key," he muttered as the engine stopped.

There were weeds growing through the gravel of the forecourt and the whole house bore witness to the decrepitude of old age. Christopher and Adam made their way up a flight of steps furnished with a once smartly painted white handrail now flecked with rust. As Christopher opened the door a musty smell filled Adam's nostrils and even in August the air seemed cool and dank.

They turned left into what had once been the study. Now a large hospital bed with a hoist filled the room, and books and papers were piled up in corners. For some reason, the linen on the bed still seemed fresh and clean, as if waiting for the occupant of the bed to return. But of course the bed would soon have to go.

They walked through into the dining room. David had clearly at some point been busy sorting out his life as there were numerous boxes marked for the charity shop or for the tip. The dining room led out into the conservatory, where once David would have looked out onto his garden, on a special armchair with legs specially raised. But now the glass of the conservatory was smudged and green, and whatever features the garden had offered were now under a thick layer of nettles, brambles and bindweed.

"Do you drink peppermint?" asked the solicitor. "I always keep a stash of teabags in my briefcase, for eventualities such as these."

Adam nodded mechanically, even though he didn't really like peppermint tea. They went into the kitchen and found a specially adapted kettle for easy pouring. Christopher rinsed out a couple of mugs and a teapot with the boiling water, then made a brew with the second kettleful. All the while Adam was silent, conscious of the ticking of the kitchen clock counting the passing minutes.

"You're still wondering why your great-uncle left you all this," Christopher continued. "In my experience there is no telling who gets chosen as the beneficiary. As they say, there's nowt as queer as folk."

"I can only imagine it was because he too was a policeman," said Adam. "But somehow that doesn't seem reason enough."

"Perhaps. Perhaps not," replied Christopher. They walked back down towards the hallway and into the lounge. David had clearly not used this room in a long while. There were piles of old papers folded back to reveal the crossword, down by the armchair, while pride of place next to the TV was a bookcase stuffed full of maps and guidebooks of European cities.

"So how long had you known David?" asked Adam, feeling that he had to push his thoughts far enough back to allow conversation.

"When he bought this house thirty-two years ago," Christopher replied. "At first I don't think he thought much of this young solicitor. It was nearly my first ever conveyancing, and I think it showed. Then he noticed my Cambridge half-blue, and we found we had a mutual interest in cricket. He hadn't played for a very long time, but he umpired occasionally. I introduced him to the local cricket club, and when he was home, we would sometimes meet up there for a chat."

"What was he like?" enquired Adam, politely sipping at his peppermint tea, and rather wishing it was something else.

"Quiet, gentle, never really pushed himself forward. He loved travelling around Europe, but he was never full of stories. I sensed he was a man of secrets somehow, but he never drew you in. He seemed quite happy being on his own, going from place to place, and then coming back here for some peace and quiet."

"Well, it's certainly not London," agreed Adam. "You know, I've sometimes dreamt of living out in the country, tending my own garden, especially when there's a really difficult case on, and you're stuck in the office watching the rain leak through the windows."

"As they say," said Christopher, "sometimes you'd better be careful what you wish for."

Adam felt this was rather a strange thing to say, even if later on those words kept coming back to him. For now he very much wanted this place to become his home, and he came to an agreement with the solicitor that he could stay here whenever he wanted, providing that he didn't dispose of anything until probate had been granted.

The peppermint tea finished, and the cups washed up, Christopher drove Adam back. They didn't go back up to the bridge and the main road. Christopher turned right past rolling parkland and the grand country home high up on a ridge, to which the avenue of lime trees had been leading. He explained the mansion had been converted into luxury flats the same time as David had bought the lodge, and the village sold to pay for death duties.

A little further on, they came across the church at the entrance to the village. "I took the liberty," said Christopher, "of arranging for you to meet the vicar and the funeral director there tomorrow. It was your great-uncle's express wish to be buried there."

Adam was slightly puzzled. All his family lived in the London area, except his parents who had now emigrated to Spain from Barking. He knew of no connection with the area, and no reason why David would wish to be buried here. Perhaps over the years he should have asked him more questions, but as Sally and Jo would often tell him, sometimes you had to stop being a detective.

And there was no doubt that the church of St Alban's, Little Netherworthy, was exceptionally pretty. Christopher stopped the car by the lychgate which led down an avenue of yews to a timeworn oak door set in a weathered sandstone south wall. Even this limited view of the church lent an air of permanence that was foreign to Adam, so used to working in a fast paced environment where change, it seemed, was the only constant.

Christopher continued down the narrow main street, which was lined with thatched cottages bearing the names of businesses that had long vanished. So the Old Post Office, for instance, stood cheek by jowl with the Old Smithy, and both seemed to be let out by a cottage holiday specialist. They reached a crossroads, and then they turned down a lane where, tucked out of view, a small estate of council houses suggested not everyone was in fact living in a rural idyll. Further on down the road they passed a scruffy farmyard full of tyres and black plastic sheeting. They had to wait while an elderly tractor pulled onto the forecourt.

From then on the lane grew narrower and twistier. They crossed the river further upstream, where Adam glimpsed what he thought was a heron, although he had never been much of a birdwatcher. The lane was climbing now, and it eventually connected up with the main road at a crossroads in one of the straggling villages they had passed earlier. "One rule," said Christopher, as they finally turned right, "never trust your Satnav round here."

Over an overcooked steak and sickly sweet Black Forest gateau, Adam attempted to process this extraordinary encounter. He had never been involved in organising a funeral before, let alone spoken with a vicar – unless you counted the one he had, as a young copper, fished out of the Thames. And then there was the house. A quick scroll through the property websites confirmed that Netherworthy Lodge would provide a decent enough deposit for a flat, but even then Adam could barely afford the mortgage. But if he didn't sell the place, what then? Was he really serious about moving one day into the country?

With all these questions going through his mind, he tried to ring his parents, but then realised it was karaoke night on the Costa Del Brit. He was aware his dad had never been that close to Uncle David. Grandad Mark, God rest his soul, thought himself a wide boy and he didn't take kindly to his kid brother being a copper – even though he was regularly ripped off by those who really knew what came off the back of a lorry. So Dad and David hadn't been close; still, Adam sent an email hoping at least for some insight as to why he had been left the entire estate.

Next he rang his big sister Sally. But it was a new school term next week, and Kai was about to start big school, and she didn't really seem that interested in his news. But then, like generations of Pennycomes before her, she had left school as soon as possible at sixteen, learnt a trade and raised a family. Mysterious relatives in Devon simply weren't part of her world, and she would probably carry on cutting hair in her salon until the very day she retired, if not longer.

That left Adam's other sister Jo. She had a complicated relationship with her parents. They had emigrated during her GSCEs, leaving her and Adam in the care of their maternal grandmother. But even before then, they had never understood why their little girl wanted to lose herself in a world of books, or why she was unable to plait her own hair or wire a plug. Adam felt deeply protective towards her, and together they naturally formed their own small dissenting faction within the wider Pennycome clan.

So Jo naturally wanted to hear all about the strange legacy, and the meeting with the vicar. And she was owed leave, so of course she would come to the funeral. She didn't, on the other hand, want to talk about the noisy neighbours, but Adam sensed she was only too glad to spend some days away from the house she was forced to share with strangers.

That left only Sadie to contact. They rarely, if ever, rang each other, and their conversation only really flowed when they were together. Yet Adam was glad of the opportunity to try and bring some order to his thoughts in an email, aware that no matter how jumbled his thoughts, Sadie always seemed to understand what he was trying to say, and how to respond.

It was getting late by now. Adam wondered how his colleagues had been getting on with the case, and whether DS Sutton had tracked down the elusive housing officer. But there were too many other questions that needed answering right now, and tomorrow he hoped at least to start finding some leads in his own very personal and very particular enquiries.

Chapter 3

ADAM BARELY SLEPT THAT NIGHT. He hadn't had much physical exercise the previous day and his mind was restless with mysteries that could not be solved. So, as soon as it was light, Adam went for a long run, along deserted streets and down country lanes, pushing himself all the while to go further, to go deeper, until at last with a clear head and aching limbs he returned to the hotel, had a long, cold shower and went off to tackle a full English, with extra toast.

It was still a couple of hours before he was due at the church, and never one to waste time, Adam drove out to the lodge to assess the state of the building. Clearly it had been neglected over the past few years, but underneath the peeling paint and odd patches of damp, the structure was generally sound. David had clearly looked after the property well, as if he knew he was soon going to have to hand on his inheritance. Yes, it needed rewiring but that was something his dad could fix next time he was over, and possibly it needed a new boiler as well, but that was well within Adam's budget. The only real issue was a large crack at the back of the double garage. Somebody had at some point built a patio or hard standing right behind it, and there was a sapling, possibly an oak, breaking through the concrete, and undermining the foundations of the wall. But even then, Adam felt sure someone with the right skills could easily fix it.

Suitably encouraged, Adam walked the short distance down the road to St Alban's. He was still early, yet the church was already open. There were two men, possibly a father and son, working on the low roof of what Adam later learnt was called the vestry. Adam called up to them, and asked if it was all right to go in. The older one nodded and Adam cautiously entered. Quite why he was so nervous he couldn't really tell. Most days he went full of confidence into all kinds of strange buildings, but that was because he had a job to do, which he usually wanted to get done as efficiently and as quickly as possible. This on the hand was a church, an alien environment, where there was no crime scene, no mystery to be solved, and time was measured more in generations than hours and minutes.

The door creaked open, and Adam stepped inside. What immediately struck him on entry was a deep sense of peace, of calm. Where that sense came from, Adam at this stage couldn't make out. He sat down in an ancient oak pew and soon realised this was a place to be, not to do. So for probably the first time in his adult life he sat, without looking at his phone, without scribbling notes on a piece of paper, without tapping his fingers impatiently waiting for the meeting to begin. As he sat, slowly, slowly his eyes adjusted to the gloom, and he realised that next to him hung the words of the Lord's Prayer painted on an ancient wooden board. Without knowing why, Adam began to read the words, as if suddenly they were all completely new and unfamiliar, and wondered what they might actually mean.

He had just reached the power and the glory when the funeral director bustled in. She was a plump, morose lady in her mid-fifties with very dry, grey hair. She only offered the briefest of introductions before making it perfectly clear she didn't usually meet clients on a Saturday, and was therefore anxious to make this meeting as brief as possible. Fortunately, Christopher, the solicitor, had provided almost all the information Adam needed, and Adam could almost hear the relief as he provided the undertaker with the clear, concise answers that she needed.

The meeting nearly over, the vicar came in, profusely apologising that he was late. At least, that is who he appeared to be from the dog collar, and the silver cross hanging round his neck. Adam, however, was expecting a typical country parson beloved of murder mysteries, with white hair, thick glasses and quite possibly a hearing aid, and he found it a real shock to be sat opposite someone in his early forties who looked like he worked out a couple of times a week and insisted on being called James.

Then, just as the funeral director was leaving, the older man who had been working on the roof also joined them. Derek, it turned out, was someone called a churchwarden, who basically kept St Alban's running. It also turned out he had known David for many years. He had roped him into various working parties, and in return had accompanied him on hikes around various nature reserves.

Adam was quickly realising how little he knew about his great-uncle, in comparison to others. He had only really seen him at family gatherings, and when occasionally he came up to Essex to visit. Since he joined the police, there had been rather more direct contact, but like many ex-coppers David rarely talked about his own personal life.

"And what about you, Revd James? How well did you know him?"

"Oh, I am still an incomer round here. In the five years since I came, I only really met him at Christmas, at Easter and on Remembrance Sunday. I knew he had been in the forces, but not much more than that."

"That's more than I knew," said Adam, trying not to sound resentful.

"Must be difficult for you," said James, who seemed to instinctively grasp the difficulty of the situation. "Then," he continued, "out of the blue, about a year ago, he asked me to come and see him. He was already waiting for a place in a home, and he knew he didn't have long left. I sensed he wanted everything sorted before he went to glory. So he gave me an order of service for his funeral, including instructions about the wake at Great Netherworthy House. He didn't really have any close family, did he?"

Adam shook his head. Somehow David knew Adam would be here, struggling to put together the pieces of his life, and again he wondered why he had been the beneficiary of such kindness. He hadn't experienced much in the way of kindness recently, and his work certainly didn't dispose him to be kind to others. All he really had to do was to fix the date, and that had already been arranged that morning. So a week on Friday it was, then – the church was booked, the vicar was free, and he simply had to turn up with, he hoped, a few others apart from Jo and Sadie.

"Shall we just run through the details, then?" asked James. But there was little really to discuss. Two hymns, "I vow to thee my country" and "Glorious things of thee are spoken"; Psalm 23 as a reading; collection to the Red Cross. The only surprise was the music going in, an Austrian folksong called Lieserl Walzer. "He said it was a reminder of his travels," explained James. Adam knew vaguely that after leaving the police David had travelled across Europe, but why this song from this country was beyond him.

"That wraps everything up, I think," said James, "unless you have any questions. At least, any questions we can answer." Again Adam shook his head. "Let's pray then," continued the vicar. Adam had never been prayed for in public before, and he assumed that at this point James would start speaking in formal Elizabethan English. But instead it was Derek who opened his mouth, and in a very simple, very straightforward way laid out the whole situation before the Lord.

"Thank you," said Adam, who at that moment wondered why he was feeling strangely emotional. He then left somewhat briskly to avoid showing any trace of emotion, and stepped out into the bright sunshine back to Little Netherworthy Lodge, his excuse being that he had to return his hire car. But in truth he wanted space to process and make decisions. A new life here would mean leaving so much behind. But then he thought of Magnolia House and the concrete wilderness that formed the backdrop to his professional career. It was safe, it was familiar, but perhaps God or Uncle David or his own gut feelings were telling him to move on. What he needed now was a week back at work to help him make up his mind.

Chapter 4

THE WEATHER BROKE ON THE Sunday evening. Dark clouds swept down from the north, blotting out the setting sun, which then swelled into large angry masses throughout the evening, until finally they burst about midnight. From his flat Adam could see lightning course across the skyline and hear the wail of emergency sirens, as blocked drains caused roads and basements to flood, and downpours found their way into tube stations, inundating tunnels and platforms. He wondered if at any moment he might be called into action, but fortunately that call never came. His shift was starting at eight, and he knew he already had a long day ahead of him.

The rain had eased off by about six, but Adam knew the public transport would still be in a state of chaos. So he set off early to walk the three or four miles to the station, trying not to get splashed by passing motorists, or to sink into oily puddles at pedestrian crossings. Even so he was fairly bedraggled by the time he arrived, and he was glad he kept a dry set of clothes at work.

By contrast DS Emma Sutton breezed in, immaculately turned out as usual, even though she had just dropped off her six year old at school. Even as she went round the team heartily greeting each member as they came into the office, DS Pennycome knew she had something important to share. Not only that, but DI Spencer, who was late again, let her take the morning briefing. It was hard for Adam at that point not to think life at Netherworthy Lodge would be better…

So, the housing manager. He had called in sick on the Wednesday and refused to take any calls. When Emma went to see him, he had just been discharged from hospital. Two lads in grey tracksuits had knocked him off his bicycle on Tuesday evening, but he would not give any further details and declined to press charges. He also refused to answer any questions about the late Mr O'connor without a solicitor present and tried to claim something about data protection when asked about the records for Magnolia House.

In the end a solicitor did turn up, and, suspecting obstruction of justice, Emma formally interviewed him under caution. She said it was like getting blood out of the proverbial stone, a sentiment shared by her rather too eager and unfortunately named sidekick DC Wayne Whittington. But in the end she ascertained a number of tenants had complained about comings and goings in Niall's flat. "And," added Wayne triumphantly, "they have all since been rehoused. The manager said it was a coincidence, but we didn't believe him, did we, Sarge?"

"So have you tracked them down?" asked Adam, who was watching the rain seep through the window frames down onto Wayne's desk.

"Er… no. That's today's job," said Wayne, "but we are making real progress."

Adam almost felt sorry for this young pup, who had only just joined the team. He exchanged a meaningful smile with his own partner, DC Stuart Sawyer, who had been nicking the bad guys from almost before the time Wayne had been born.

Just then the telephone in DI Spencer's office rang. "Hold that thought," he said, "that's probably forensics telling me the results are on their way."

As expected, Niall had died from an overdose of heroin cut with caffeine. The heroin came from the same batch so carefully wrapped under his bed, which at least suggested there was plenty more out there. Analysis of his stomach contents showed that his last meal had been fish and chips washed down with Coke. That in itself might not have been too significant, but the residues of cooking oil on the cash and the stash, and minute food particles indicated some connection with a fast food outlet. In addition, the clingfilm wrapping the items was culinary grade and it showed distinctive perforation marks from the particular cutter used to tear it.

That, at least, was the positive news. There were no clear sets of fingerprints that could be recovered from the suitcases, and whoever did the work probably wore disposable gloves. There was limited evidence from the rest of the flat, as well. Clearly there had been plenty of people going out over a long period of time, and working out who was there when would be an almost impossible task.

"So where do we go from here?" asked Wayne, with his customary, and at least to Adam, annoying enthusiasm.

"You and Emma are already following up the ex-tenants," said DI Spencer. "That leaves Adam and Stuart. So, your mission, should you choose to accept it, is to check out local takeaways within, say, a two mile radius of the deceased's flat."

"It's a tough gig," observed Stuart drily, "but someone's got to do it."

"Not without a risk assessment," replied Adam smiling.

"What do you mean?" asked Wayne.

"If I go down with food poisoning, I am going to sue. I had a bad experience with a kebab shop near there when I first became a detective," laughed Adam. "OK, seriously, Stuart, let's work out how we are going to do this. And Wayne, you better move your stuff away from the windows. The rain's not going to stop any time soon."

Emma glared at him, not only, Adam suspected, because he was teasing her protégé, but because, in the excitement of the forensics report, her big reveal had almost been ignored. But Adam pretended not to notice. Soon he was deep in conversation with Stuart, drawing a circle on a map, and working out a timetable for the next few days.

Adam eventually found what he was looking for on Wednesday evening. He had agreed with Stuart a couple of undercover detectives turning up at a takeaway together would attract more suspicion, so Stuart worked on the side of the railway line bordering Magnolia House, while Adam worked on the other side.

Great Jones Street was an impressive row of restored Georgian townhouses, with solid, freshly painted front doors, unsuccessfully attempting to hide the obvious wealth behind them. But Adam was not there to admire the architecture. Halfway down the length of the street ran a small stone wall, with immaculately tended flower beds, marking the end of affluence. Beyond, and only accessible by the narrowest of cut-throughs, was the postwar estate built over the ruins of the other half of the street. It was a maze of maisonettes and terraced houses, set around narrow streets never designed for motor cars – which was one reason why Adam was on foot. And there in the middle was a shopping arcade now hosting a betting shop, a convenience store, various charity shops and right at the end the Great Jones Fish Fryer.

Adam knew it was the place the moment he saw the youths in grey hoodies hanging around outside. He had a hunch, but nothing more, that these were the ones responsible for mugging the housing manager. As soon as they saw Adam, they briefly turned away from the girls they were hanging with, and started talking on their phones. Whether it was because they suspected Adam was a copper, or because no-one ever came through from the other side, he couldn't rightly say.

For a Wednesday evening in August, the chip shop was surprisingly quiet. There were just a few elderly folk collecting their regular orders, and grumbling about the sharp shower that had just started outside.

"Whaddya want?" asked a young woman in an Arsenal shirt and greasy apron from behind the counter. She was smiling as she said it, but it was clear Adam in his cotton shirt and pressed trousers did not inspire a lot of trust.

"A small cod and chips," replied Adam, "no salt, no vinegar," remembering the contents of Niall's stomach.

"Coming right up," said the lass, using a turn of phrase that right at that moment Adam found rather unfortunate, "and anything else?"

"Yeah, can you wrap up a cheeseburger for my mate? It's rather minging, but he likes to eat them cold for supper."

"Oi, Grease," said the assistant shouting out the back, "can you do us a cheeseburger?"

The aforementioned Grease appeared for a moment in the doorway. Adam saw a tall, powerfully built lad, his fair, cropped hair hidden under his hat, with piercing blue eyes and thin, pale lips. "No problemo," he said, glancing at Adam with what Adam could only describe as a cold look of suspicion.

A few minutes later Adam crossed back through the cut-through. He wondered how many residents on this side had takeaways for supper, and he noticed a disdainful look from a fragrant lady in a designer outfit who brushed past him. But Adam had no intention of eating his purchase. The last two days had only increased his loathing for fast food, and besides, he was gathering evidence. When he finally reached his car, he placed the offending items in an evidence bag and made his way back to the station.

It was Adam's turn to lead the briefing the following morning. DS Sutton and DC Whittington had had a lot of trouble finding the former tenants, and not one of them was willing to elaborate on their previous complaints.

"At least you have corroborated the forensic evidence that there were plenty of people coming and going," said Adam, "the question is, who?"

"So, let me introduce you to Great Jones Chip Fryer. DI Spencer is leaning on forensics to produce the goods by the end of tomorrow." DI Spencer nodded and Adam wished at this point he didn't have to take next week off. "As I approached, I noticed various points of interest. First, the gang of youths in grey tracksuits. They didn't seem to be there by chance, and as soon as they saw me, they started talking on their phones. Secondly, the comprehensive CCTV system covering the front of the shop. Thirdly, the thickness of the front door and the shuttering system. I did not have opportunity to look round the side or the back of the building, but either we have a very security conscious chip shop owner, or someone who wants to keep something hidden."

"But how does this relate to Magnolia House?" asked Wayne.

"Good question," replied Adam. "There's an underpass running almost directly into the Great Jones estate. It has been the scene of various muggings over the past few months, all of them open cases."

"I'm going to go through them this morning," said Stuart, "to see if there's any pattern."

"Don't forget to talk to PC McQueen and her colleagues," said DI Spencer. "And, Adam, if your hunch is correct, we need to know how the hell this operation has been allowed to operate under our nose, and for how long. So look into the owner, see what you can find out. But don't go too deep before we get forensics, it could just be you're barking up the wrong tree."

"We have a near fatal stabbing that came in last night," said Emma, "so Wayne and I will get onto that."

"Agreed," said DI Spencer, "but I have a feeling if Adam's right, we're all going to get involved, one way or another."

Adam spent the rest of the morning sat at his desk, writing up paperwork and tracking down the proprietor of the chip shop. Eventually he came up with a name – Stan Collins. In his typically methodical fashion he then looked into Mr Collins' criminal record. Four offences of possession, nothing, however, relating to intent to supply. That surprised Adam. So, wondering if for a moment his hunch had somehow let him down, he looked at the convictions in more detail. That was when he realised something was wrong, seriously wrong.

DI Spencer would not be back until later. He was on yet more diversity and equality training, which as Adam wryly noted, was just what you needed in the middle of a major investigation. Bearing in mind the warning not to go in too deep, he wandered over to Stuart to see what his review of the muggings had turned up.

Stuart Sawyer always gave the impression of being an easy going, affable grandfather and he made no secret he was looking forward to retirement in a couple of years' time in order to spend more time with his family. But Adam soon learnt after joining the unit that underneath this placid exterior was a man who prized loyalty, service and commitment. He thought little of career officers who would do almost anything to gain a promotion, and he expected respect for his many years of hard, honest labour. And even though Adam had recently been promoted, he certainly gave that respect, and saw in Stuart someone who in many ways was a kindred spirit.

"How are you getting on?" asked Adam, bringing over a mug of coffee as a token of esteem – three sugars, with only a dash of milk.

"Well," said Stuart, sighing, "there's not that much to go on. The victims haven't exactly provided a lot of detail. But there's fair mention of our friends in grey tracksuits, and most of the attacks involved the theft of a phone."

"That's suggestive at least," said Adam and Stuart nodded. "You want to be in this drug business? Fine, first prove yourself and nick a phone. I can see plenty of lads who might well want to take up the challenge."

"Or lasses," said DI Spencer, who was coming in through the door, "we of course can't assume how they will identify themselves."

"No, of course not," said Adam, "and what is your preferred pronoun today?"

"Don't ask," said DI Spencer, clearly relieved to be back. "What's come in while I've been out?"

"I need a quiet word," said Adam, changing the mood in an instance.

"OK, in my office in half an hour. Lunch has to be my first priority."

It was, however, nearer half three when Adam finally got to speak with his boss. Quite rightly, DS Sutton wanted to brief about the stabbing, and then Stuart was called out to another case that had just been reported.

"So, what's up?" said DI Spencer as Adam shut the door and squeezed into the chair that just fitted on the other side of the desk.

"First of all, does the name Stan Collins mean anything to you?"

DI Spencer shook his head. "Should it?"

"Not particularly. His only convictions were for possession, never for intent to supply."

"So, why should I be interested?" The inspector had clearly had a frustrating day so far, and he certainly didn't want to listen to minor details.

"Our Mr Collins is the proprietor of the Great Jones Fish Fryer and in every case the arresting officer was Carl Carter."

"Oh shit," said DI Sutton.

"That was my reaction," said Adam. DS Carter had left the unit just before Adam had arrived. There were all kinds of rumours as to why he had left but no specific reason had ever been given. All Adam knew is that he went to work as a security consultant on the Costa del Brit but then died in a road accident a year later.

"If your hunch about the chip shop is wrong, I will tear up my Brentford season ticket."

"Steady on, sir. You don't want to do anything you'll later regret."

"No, but I am going to make sure forensics gives us those results tomorrow. And I will put some feelers to see if you can access DS Carter's records. Something found here stinks, and it's not just the evidence you brought back last night. In the meantime, you can't mention this to anyone else. Understood?"

Adam nodded.

"You've gone as far as you can for now. I suggest you join DC Sawyer for the rest of the day and focus on something else. Until we get forensics, the case is purely circumstantial."

Adam nodded again and headed out to the domestic Stuart was investigating. It was a fairly straightforward case and by nine o'clock they had tracked down and apprehended the chief suspect.

"You sometimes wish every case was like this, don't you?" said Stuart as they returned to an otherwise empty office.

"I dunno," said Adam, "where would the fun be?" It was a casual, throwaway remark made without much thought, but it was one that would stick with Adam in the weeks and months ahead. "But there's still paperwork to do... Are you OK to write it up? I need to go home and make a phone call."

"Sure," said Stuart, smiling wearily, "I have already rung the missus." It was the sort of conversation Adam realised his constable must have made hundreds of times before. As he tidied his desk and put on his jacket, he couldn't help thinking of Sadie. If indeed, their relationship ever reached that point.

But tonight, there was other business to attend to. After a quick supper (Adam discovered the local supermarket had frying steak on special offer), he picked up the phone to his father.

"Hello, son," Dad said in his usual jaunty Essex accent. "How's you doing?"

"Not bad. And you?"

"Yeah, yeah, I'm fine. Bit worried about Mum though. She's started drinking again."

"I didn't know she stopped."

"Well, yeah, she did. She tries hard, you know."

But it's hard when the man you love always has a bit on the side, thought Adam. There was an awkward silence for a moment, while Adam and his dad both processed what the other was thinking.

"Sorry I didn't get back to you about the funeral. I have a big job on, installing floodlights down the golf course."

"You said you were retired, at least, how did you put it, semi-retired?"

"Son, the money don't stretch like it used to. And besides, folk round here are looking for someone who does an honest job, if you know what I mean."

Adam smiled. Even in Spain, his father's prejudice against foreigners was as strong as ever. Not that he ever really did or understood irony.

"I might have some work for you," Adam said, changing the subject, "I've been looking at Uncle David's house. It probably needs completely rewiring, certainly it needs a lot more sockets."

"What? You're not going to live in that old pile, are you?"

"Might do, I haven't decided yet."

"Son, you have had some pretty strange ideas, ever since you went to university. But that I have to say is the strangest I have heard yet."

Adam realised if he wasn't quick, he would hear the whole spiel about the university of life, and they would probably end up in a pointless argument, yet again.

"Anyway," said Adam, "there's another reason why I rang. Did you ever bump into someone called Carl Carter?"

"Who wants to know? Oh wait, you can't tell me. Yeah, I met him a few times down the golf course. Way too flash ever to have been a policeman. Always wondered where he got that much dosh from."

"Go on," said Adam, and Dad needed no second invitation. "The Rolex, the Aviator sunglasses, the tailor made shirts. He wasn't living off a policeman's pension, was he? I made a few enquiries, if you know what I mean. Nobody knew the security business he did, but it paid well. I can tell you that."

"That's really helpful," said Adam. He steered the conversation round to the football, not wanting to divulge any details, and soon they were setting to rights the new season that had just gotten underway. Then Adam noticed the time. He wanted to speak to Mum, but she had gone to bed as she was feeling unwell, and Adam again wondered what was really going on.

After he hung up, he then checked his personal emails. A cousin of Uncle David had got in touch to say he and his family would be attending the funeral. Adam racked his brains, but only the dimmest recollection from his grandfather's funeral came to mind. Still, it was good to know there would at least be other family there, and he wrote a polite reply, all the while wondering if the floodlights on the golf course were a reason or an excuse.

Then there was the draft order of service sent by the funeral director to the vicar and himself. As Adam checked it carefully, he thought of the little church and that overwhelming sense of peace he had experienced there. Was it possible the same God was with him in the overwhelming busyness of his daily life? That was a question Adam felt unqualified to answer. But, as he reflected on the events of that long Thursday, it would do no harm, he reckoned, to pray that the results of the forensics tomorrow would be as he expected.

Adam made a few corrections, pressed send, and then found he was reciting the words of the Lord's Prayer. Whether that made any difference, well, that would be seen tomorrow.

Chapter 5

ADAM WALKED TO WORK AGAIN that morning. He was anxious to discover the results of the forensics and he knew that sitting on a bus would only leave him even more wound up and irritable. Fortunately, this time it was dry, and there was a cooling east wind which took the edge off the heat in the city. He found himself wondering what the weather would be like in Little Netherworthy and whether he would miss the relentless tide of traffic slowly crawling into the city today, and the pungent smell of exhaust fumes – assuming, of course, that he would ever move there. One thing, to be sure, it would certainly be less dangerous. He paused briefly to aid a cyclist who had been clipped by a passing wing mirror, and after checking no real damage had been done, hastened for the last half a mile into the station.

Stuart, as might be expected, was a few minutes' late after last night's efforts. But professional as ever, he set himself straight to business. He and Adam reviewed the details of the domestic and prepared for the interview. There was a problem finding a duty solicitor but eventually one rolled up just after ten and the usual formalities of a no comment question and answer session, as well as the reading of a prepared statement, were all impeccably observed. It was a process everyone in the room knew well, and after it was over, the suspect went back to his cell, Adam and Stuart prepared to contact the CPS, and the duty solicitor went off to another interview room and to another uncommunicative client. It was as routine a morning as Adam ever experienced in his line of work, and today was the day he needed routine.

After the CPS had agreed that charges should be brought, the suspect was remanded into custody, and it was lunchtime. Stuart was going to take the afternoon off, and although Adam was hungry, he also was keen to keep his mind occupied. So after grabbing a sandwich and a pork pie, he sat down with DC Whittington – DS Sutton was out testifying in court – and helped to review the CCTV in the stabbing case. He still remembered how in his first days in the unit he had had to spend hours in front of a screen, trying to make out fuzzy grey and white images, and even for someone like Wayne it was hard not to feel a certain amount of sympathy.

They had just come to some crucial pictures from a garage forecourt, when DI Spencer emerged from his office. "It's come through?" said Adam.

DI Spencer nodded, "I've sent the report to your computer."

As expected, the perforations on the clingfilm matched the perforations on the wrappings in the suitcases under the bed. Not only that, but the chips retrieved from the deceased's stomach had been cut in the same way as the chips Adam had put in the evidence bag. Not even the most skilled defence lawyer could now deny there was a definite and concrete connection between the death in Magnolia House and the Great Jones Fish Fryer.

"So how did you know your hunch would be correct?" asked Wayne, who was still glued to his photos.

"I prayed," said Adam, laughing – yet at the same time not sure if he was serious, "or at least I used my experience to make an educated guess."

"Better pray we find enough resources to keep the premises under surveillance," said DI Spencer. "I've just spent the last hour talking resources with those higher up. They all agree we can't just go marching in, until we know what we are dealing with, and who might be behind this operation. What they can't agree is where we'll find the money and the resources to carry out a full-scale surveillance operation. I have been told the boys from the Drugs Squad may help us. But they are stretched as we are, so it looks like overtime all round, I'm afraid."

"I needn't go on Monday," said Adam.

"No, you go," said DI Spencer. "Family comes first. You know me – firm but fair."

Wayne smiled at Adam. For all his inexperience, he had already cottoned on to the governor's favourite phrase.

"Meanwhile," said DI Spencer, "there's the other matter you brought up, Adam. For that, I need you in my office."

Adam shut the door behind him, and his eyes had to adjust momentarily to the artificial light inside.

"So I have been talking to personnel. They were very reluctant to let me have any information at first. But they have let me have some very edited details of the late Carl Carter, on the provision I kept them here on my computer and did not share them with anybody."

"Understood."

"For the next few minutes you can have the immense privilege of sitting on my side of the desk, while I go and find a healthy dose of vitamin D. I think I can trust you with my computer."

Adam smiled. "Your files on Brentford FC are no concern of mine, I can assure you."

As soon as DI Spencer left, Adam eased himself into the worn leather chair that creaked alarmingly as he sat on it. He opened the file and then he stopped himself. The first picture was of a young PC Carter just after joining the force, and Adam knew instantly where he had seen that face before: the fair hair, the piercing blue eyes, the thin, pale lips. This was Grease he was looking at, and unless there had been some freak genetic accident, Carter and Grease were related, if not father and son. He ploughed on into the file, hoping to find more information, but just as he was told, the file had been heavily redacted, and if there had been any disciplinary offences he certainly was not privileged to see him.

Adam waited for DI Will Spencer to return. There was a cheap wall clock loudly marking the passing of the minutes. He thought for a moment of the still, peaceful church in Little Netherworthy, and found that he was restlessly tapping his fingers, waiting any moment for the door to open.

"Found anything useful?" said DI Spencer, bearing two cups of coffee.

"Nothing I can prove," said Adam, "but you might want to put those cups down before I go any further."

Adam felt very conscious of being on the wrong side of the desk, as if the order of his daily life had been momentarily turned upside down. Was this a seat he would one day sit in? He wasn't sure, and at the moment he had rather more pressing concerns.

"So," said Adam turning round the monitor, "this is PC Carter."

"Yep," said Will, "I know that face well. I have been tempted before to punch it."

"I've seen that face as well. At the Great Jones Fish Fryer."

"Sorry," said Will, "you've lost me."

"There's a young lad who works out the back. I just caught a glimpse of him, as I placed my order. But he looked at me, and I looked at him. And he is the spitting image of our mutual friend."

"I need my coffee," said Will, who took a deep slurp and thought for a moment.

"You may say it's just my hunch. But I think at the very least I need to find out who Grease is, and whether there's a connection."

"I will have a discreet word with personnel," said Will, "but I doubt they will be able to tell us anything. In the meanwhile, can you avoid having any more hunches for today?"

"Just ask personnel if I can keep this picture," said Adam, getting up. "I'm off to do some digging. And thanks for the coffee, by the way."

"You're welcome," said DI Spencer, resuming his normal position on the other side of the desk.

At that moment DS Sutton rang up to say she was going straight from court to pick up her son from the childminder. In one sense, Adam was relieved. There was no way of knowing how she would have reacted if she had walked in on Adam in DI Spencer's seat. But her absence meant he would have to spend the rest of the afternoon helping Wayne with the stabbing case. That, Adam, realised was right and proper – hard evidence had to come before hunches. But at the same time he knew it was going to be a long weekend following up his own particular leads – even if, as was unlikely, no other cases came in. So, with a certain feeling of reluctance, he made two cups of coffee and headed over to Wayne's desk.

Fortunately, it turned out that for all his puppyish qualities, Wayne was a willing grafter and keen learner, and by eight o'clock they had together made good progress. "Fancy a curry, sir?" asked Wayne as they decided then was a good time to stop.

"So tell me a little about your family," said Adam, as they tucked into tikka masala and poppadoms.

"There's not much to say," said Wayne, "Mum and Dad divorced but still good friends, brother, sister, two dogs, and two sets of grandparents still alive and reasonably healthy."

"No family secrets?" asked Adam, trying not to turn yet another conversation into an interrogation.

"Nope, nothing as far as I'm aware. What about you?"

"Not quite sure, I'll keep you posted."

"Ah, a family mystery. I can see that'll be right up your street."

"Hmm," said Adam, not wishing to divulge anything further. As he dipped his poppadom into the sauce, he couldn't help thinking that in a week's time he would be with Sadie and Jo, and he could have a proper conversation. Still, he had to make do with what was in front of him, and Wayne knew enough about football and cricket to stave off any awkward pauses. So fighting off the loneliness, the rest of the evening passed fairly pleasantly and at the end he felt magnanimous enough to pay for the both of them.

But as Adam walked home, he could sense a certain impatience niggling away at him, and as soon as he was able, he went into the office the next morning, anxious to start digging. So first of all who was Grease? He tracked down the payroll records for the fish and chip shop. Not surprisingly, there was no-one with the surname Carter. So he then checked up on the three men who worked there. Two of them had criminal records and Grease was clearly neither of them. By a process of elimination, that left the one individual Lewis Sinclair.

But who was this Lewis Sinclair? On, then, to birth certificates and electoral registers. Lewis Sinclair had been born twenty-four years ago – that would be about right, judging from their brief encounter. Only the mother's name was recorded on his certificate, and that was no real surprise. So what could he find out about Carol Sinclair?

There were plenty of women who bore the same name, but some very patient detective work eventually identified the right one. She was, to no great surprise, living on the Great Jones estate. She appeared to have only the one child, and Lewis lived with her until he was about eight. And then this same Carol Sinclair suddenly vanished from the records. Adam hunted and hunted for some trace of her, but from that point on it was as if she never existed.

Adam was starting to get a bad feeling about Carol. Who would simply leave an eight year old child behind? And what would drive a woman to such an extreme measure? He couldn't help thinking about Carl Carter and wondering about the exact nature of her relationship with him. But there was also a little boy who needed looking after. What was he learning at this age? And was he safe?

Further trawling led to the discovery that Lewis Sinclair spent his teenage years living with Stan Collins, and at least for some of the time, Stan's partner Gloria McNeil. Now this was getting seriously messy. What kind of relationship did Stan have with Lewis? And why did no-one question the arrangement? Unfortunately, Carl Carter couldn't provide those answers as he had now moved permanently to a new address underground.

Adam needed another coffee. As he got up, DC Maria Watson came over to consult him about a piece of evidence she was processing. She had just returned from maternity leave and was working weekends while her partner looked after the baby. Maybe she was just rusty, or more likely, deprived of sleep, but the query was very easily solved. So once that was sorted, they chatted for a few moments over a brew, about nothing very much, and Adam sensed she was glad of some grown up talk.

It was as they were talking about favourite Italian dishes, that something in the back of Adam's mind tripped an internal alarm switch. He made his apologies and went back to the payroll records of the fish and chip shop. Yes, there was a McNeil working there, and not only that but Shania McNeil had convictions for handling stolen goods. So was Shania related to Gloria? Yes, they were – she was Gloria's daughter, and here Adam wrote a big question mark, quite possibly Lewis' step-sister.

Whatever was going down on that particular estate, it seemed to Adam he was tugging away at the very outer edge of a large spider's web. He was getting hungry by now, but he wanted to keep on working.

So, first of all, who had arrested Shania McNeil? He looked at the name of the officer in question – DC Frank Fogarty. That meant nothing. So he carried out a quick online search, to see what he could find out. Very soon he discovered DC Frank Fogarty had been accused of rape, but in court he was cleared partly on the evidence of guess who? The spider at the centre of the web, DS Carl Carter.

Adam was rapidly filling a notebook but there was more to come. For a quick check of Shania's address revealed she was living on the second floor of guess where? Lilac House. At this point, Adam immediately thought of PC Blessing McQueen's words about a curtain moving. He couldn't prove it, but he sensed it was more than likely Shania was keeping an eye on events across the courtyard in Magnolia House. And there was CCTV from Lilac House.

So after a brief interlude for a sausage roll and chips, Adam sat down for the afternoon with the CCTV from the doorway. DC Stuart Sawyer had already reviewed it, but Adam was now looking at it with fresh eyes. Forensics had identified the time of Niall O'connor's death somewhere between 10pm and midnight that Tuesday. So who was going in or out around that time or shortly afterwards? At 1.03am there came the answer. A young woman emerged, and although it was a hot, sticky night, she was concealing her face with a hoodie. She was carrying a plastic bag, and as she passed through the door, something slid out. Adam zoomed in, and although the image wasn't very clear, it looked like a roll of disposable cloths.

Who would go out in the middle of the night to do some cleaning? wondered Adam, already knowing the answer. Twenty-two minutes later, the young woman returned. The heat had obviously got to her, and she was carrying the hoodie over her bag, perhaps to keep one hand free, perhaps to conceal what was in the bag. Either way, there was no denying the woman in question was Shania McNeil.

There still wasn't enough to build a case, of course, and it was vitally important that no-one tugged at the web too hard unless it broke, and everyone caught up in it managed to run away. But Adam was content enough. He had at last obtained some definite evidence, and now alone in the office, he wrote up his report and left it prominently positioned on DI Spencer's desk, as if giving a going away present for his boss to open on Monday morning. Then he turned off the lights and left.

Chapter 6

THAT MONDAY MORNING ADAM DECIDED to travel down from London in a hire car. Adam generally enjoyed driving, but there was little point owning a car in the capital, so in the usual course of business he relied on buses and taxis to get around. As he ground his way slowly onto the motorway, he did, however, begin to regret his decision. It was an unseasonably hot September day; tempers on the road were frayed, and if he had been a traffic cop, he would have been more than tempted to have a word with some of his fellow travellers.

He had decided that if he was going to use the few days as holiday, he would travel cross-country. Only there had been a coach fire somewhere along the A303, and after an hour stuck in a traffic jam, he found himself travelling round parts of Wiltshire and Dorset he barely knew existed, on single carriageway roads that only grudgingly wound round to the right direction. The heat by now was intense, and a scorching wind flung dust and dirt over the car windscreen. Adam pulled over at a filling station to clean the glass, even though he knew that ultimately his actions were futile. Then he picked up a can of Red Bull and went on his way.

It was nearly four o'clock when Adam finally turned up at the solicitors. Christopher Brunt had already left the office, and a bored receptionist handed him the keys to the lodge with only the barest acknowledgement. Adam was by now desperate to arrive and to get some exercise, but first there was still the short but twisty journey out to Netherworthy Lodge. A school bus stopped in one of the villages to unload a solitary student; a little further on an elderly lady tottered uncertainly across a pedestrian crossing; there were building materials being unloaded from a lorry parked in front of him.

It was a relief indeed when Adam found the turning down to the lodge. Yet even as Adam got out of the car, he was suddenly struck by the absurdity of the situation. Here was an unknown property in an unfamiliar place owned by a relative he barely knew. And now it was, or would surely become, his. Looking at the situation from a purely professional point of view, such an act of generosity by his great-uncle made no sense. Indeed, Adam had to admit that part of him was actually suspicious of the whole business. But then again, as Sadie and Jo often pointed out, there were times when you had to stop suspecting and start trusting. And maybe, just maybe, this gift was a simple act of affection from someone who – as far as he could tell – had no family to speak of.

With conflicting emotions, therefore, Adam turned the key and once more he was struck how the lodge provided a relief from the heat outside. Surrounded by a high laurel hedge, and sheltered by the ridge of land rising up behind the copse, the house afforded natural protection from whatever was happening in the wider world. He dumped his bags in the first bedroom, and then, as agreed with the solicitors, he read the meters. It was only then it dawned on him that there was no mobile signal, and of course Uncle David had lived without the Internet.

In that moment Adam felt very cut off, very isolated from the 24/7 way of life he had enjoyed ever since his schooldays, and suddenly the prospect of spending the next few days in complete isolation seemed completely overwhelming. One of his secret fears had always been ending up in a prison cell without any means of communication. Now it seemed that fear was about to be realised.

So Adam got busy. He had bought a few basics with him from home, in order to clean the house from top to bottom. But now he realised he was hungry, and it wasn't as if he could simply walk out to the nearest supermarket. Fortunately, he remembered there was a garden centre with a farm shop just beyond the turning to the lodge, and even though it was about to close, he was able to pick up some artisan bread, and other overpriced staples that would tide him over until morning. There was also a signal there, so he messaged Jo and Sadie, and talked to the Internet provider who unfortunately could only sort something out within the next month.

Adam could feel the frustration in him boiling over. If everything was sorted, he would have gone for a long run. For now, it was the kitchen and the bathroom that bore the brunt of his aggression. There was mould to remove, grease to dissolve, surfaces to be disinfected, crockery and cutlery – a total collection of oddments – to be washed up or thrown, floors to be mopped, cupboards stripped and sorted.

As Adam plunged into his work, he realised he needed some music to keep him company. He went into the lounge where he found a CD player and a collection of discs. Intriguingly he found they were mostly of American blues artists, with strange sounding names like Leadbelly and Maceo Merryweather and Big Bill Broonzy. Adam wondered how and where his Great-Uncle David had acquired such musical tastes, and as he tackled the years of benign neglect, he tried to imagine a retired cop from London sitting in his house in Devon listening to the plaintive sounds of the American working class. Somehow it just didn't seem to fit. Clearly there was more, much more to find out.

It was half past seven by the time Adam stopped for a bite to eat. He was glad of the break, but he was not yet ready to confront the silence in the house. So after putting everything away in the newly cleaned fridge, he went upstairs with the CD player and with the blues still playing in the background he began to investigate the bedrooms, to see what he could find out.

The answer was not very much. Much of the contents of the boxes destined for the charity shop and the tip had clearly come from here. There were bare mattresses in all three bedrooms, waiting for someone to come and set up home, and Adam was grateful he had at least remembered to bring bed linen and towels for himself.

The only obvious reminder of the person who used to live here were a couple of photographs in the bedroom where Adam had dumped his bag. One Adam realised was of his grandfather Mark as a boy with his younger brother, and the other must have been of the boys' parents on their wedding day. But those yielded no clues at all about David's life as an adult. Frustrated, Adam began to explore further.

The second bedroom provided little, if any, new information. The outdoor clothes in the wardrobe confirmed only what Adam had seen from some of the books and maps downstairs, namely that David had enjoyed hiking and birdwatching. The carpet here was particularly faded and worn, and Adam made a mental note to add this to the growing list of things to be sorted.

It was only the third bedroom which at last yielded some secrets. Adam had expected somewhere to find souvenirs of David's life as a policeman, and indeed here were his badge and helmet carefully wrapped away along with his service record. There were also several photos of colleagues in grainy black and white, and a few newspaper articles which mentioned David by name. Adam thought back to that last conversation in a nursing home, and it was clear to him that David had worn his badge with pride. Yet Adam also knew his uncle's career as a copper had only been one part of his life. So, he wondered, what else could there be?

As Adam continued to rummage through the cupboard, his attention was drawn to the red cap on the top shelf. He instantly recognised it as belonging to the Royal Military Police. What was it that the vicar had said about David always coming to Remembrance Sunday? This was a part of David's life his father had never mentioned, perhaps because it simply never interested him. The photos on this shelf were older and many showed a city somewhere overseas bearing the scars of war. As Adam leafed through the album he caught the name, "Graz", which didn't mean a lot to him. But perhaps it explained to some degree why David so enjoyed travelling round Europe on business. With his sense of mystery heightened, Adam moved on to discover David's military record. It showed that at the age of 18, in 1948, he had joined up and after three years serving in Yorkshire had been posted with the British Occupation Force in Austria for a further four. Apparently, according to a map carefully folded up with the papers, this city called Graz was at the centre of the British Zone.

At this point Adam really wished he could log onto the Internet and find out more. He hadn't ever realised that the British had occupied part of Austria, and he had no idea what they were doing out there. Adam continued to search. He found a bundle of postcards, and an invitation to a 50th reunion ceremony in Graz. There was also an address book with the names of several old comrades, although Adam noted several of them had since been crossed out – casualties no doubt, like David, of the last enemy, death itself. Adam tucked the book into his pocket and made a mental note to contact those who were apparently still alive.

As he went back downstairs he decided on a whim to phone his sister Jo. She was that rare breed, a German linguist, and next to the Internet she was probably his best source of information. There was still a landline in the house, and the solicitor had thoughtfully arranged for its reconnection. So Adam rang, and rang, until finally there was an answer.

"Hello?" said Jo, who was clearly suspicious of a number she didn't recognise. Her voice sounded tired and thin.

"Is everything all right?" Adam asked.

"You know those neighbours I was talking about…" Jo replied, and her voice tailed off. "Sorry, I haven't slept properly for a week. And work's a beast at the moment."

Adam thought for a moment. "Call round at the station and ask for PC Nicky Nicholls at the front desk. He has a set of my flat keys. You can doss down there until I come back."

"You sure?"

"Absolutely," Adam replied. Although Jo was only eighteen months younger, Adam had spent most of his school days looking out for his little sister. Being Jo wasn't cool, and other kids let her know it. And even now he was more than willing to play the part of big brother when needed.

"You haven't said why you've rung," said Jo after a short pause.

"Well, it's nothing really," replied Adam. "Have you heard of a place called Graz?"

"It's pronounced Gr-aa-ts," said Jo. "You were always rubbish at languages, weren't you?"

"Oui, madame."

"So what do you want to know? Second largest city in Austria, population of 250,000, believe it's a really nice place."

"Did you know it was home to the British Occupation Force after the war?"

"Yes, that's right. Just like Germany, Austria was divided among the four allied powers, and Graz was the centre of British operations."

"Did you know Uncle David was a military policeman out there?"

"No, I didn't," said Jo, "Mum and Dad never said. But it would kind of make sense."

"What do you mean?"

"You remember the only time David stayed with us? I think I was about six. Mum and Dad went out for the evening, and I couldn't sleep. I went downstairs to find Uncle David. Don't know why, I'm not sure he ever knew what to do with children. But I put my head in his lap, and he began to stroke my hair and speak a poem in a language I had never heard before. I didn't know it was German. But I loved the sounds, and later on when I had that German schoolfriend, she helped me learn it. I was so happy I could say the poem I rushed home and told it to Mum and Dad. Dad shouted at me, mentioned the war, and that was the reason why Uncle David never stayed again. And why my German friend was never invited round to my house."

"But you went on to study German anyway."

"Yeah," said Jo, sounding a little brighter. "My act of teenage rebellion. All thanks to Uncle David." "I never knew," said Adam.

"I don't think you'd have understood. Besides, the only things that really interested you were cricket and football."

"And that girl in your class."

"I wasn't going to bring that up," said Jo.

Adam and Jo chatted for a little longer, and when he had hung up, Adam suddenly became aware of the great silence in the house. Usually by this stage of the evening he would be online or streaming a film or out at a curry house. But tonight he was completely alone. It was just him and a house of only partially discovered memories.

It was still only half nine. There was only a very limited selection of channels on television, but Adam needed the distraction of something on in the background. Eventually, he admitted defeat and went to bed about midnight. But in the heavy, warm silence of an early September night, he found his dreams were filled with too many images from recent crime scenes: the photos he had used against a notorious local paedophile; the all too real body found stabbed and bloodied in a local park; the child whose unexplained disappearance still festered as a wound deep inside him.

So Adam ran. With only a headtorch to light the way, he pounded the dark country lanes, taking care to note the route he was taking. Further and further he ran, pushing his body to its absolute limit, the echo of his footsteps the only sound that disturbed the thick night air. At one point he rounded a bend and disturbed a deer, but she melted away into the shadows; in a hamlet, peaceful and still, a fox ambled past quite nonchalantly on his nightly rounds. Adam, however, barely noticed these sights. He wanted to focus only on the physical sensation of putting one leg in front of the other, the taking of breath, the sweat trickling down his back. Eventually and reluctantly he reached his limit and made his way back, to sleep in a deep, dark place, free of nightmares, until the mid-morning sun finally woke him up.

Adam stretched and contemplated the coming day. He had a list of tasks to do, and another of items that needed purchasing. But first, he needed to complete the inspection of the property, to see what he might have missed. He could tell even just looking out of his bedroom window the weeds and bushes had overtaken the garden. That was the sort of job for Sadie, he decided, and he knew how much she would throw herself into the project. But what else was there still to discover?

The solicitor had mentioned something about a couple of cars in the garage, and about one of them being a classic. That had been enough to attract Adam's interest, although when he made his way past the boxes meant for the charity shop he was slightly disappointed only to find a Nissan Micra. Still once it was back on the road, it would be fine as a runaround, and a quick telephone call confirmed that the local dealer would be happy to collect and service it.

But as Adam was beginning to realise, there was often more in Uncle David's life than met the eye, and sure enough, next to it was a large vehicle covered in a tarpaulin. Intrigued he lifted the covers, and found himself looking at an early 80s steel-blue Granada estate. Why his Great-Uncle David had kept it was beyond him. It had come apparently from a garage called Fairhurst Motors, but Adam was pretty sure it had long gone out of business, probably around the same time David had stopped driving the motor. However, the old lady seemed to be in decent enough condition, and the contact at the Nissan dealership mentioned someone out in the wilds who could possibly restore it.

That was the good news. The bad news was the state of the garage itself. Adam had already seen the crack in the back wall from the outside, and the sapling breaking through the hard standing. From the inside a closer inspection revealed this was a job that needed tackling, and soon. Some of the breeze blocks were starting to jut out of true, and the cement holding them in place was cracking. But who did Adam know who could do the work?

On a whim, Adam walked purposefully down to the church. He thought maybe there would be a notice somewhere advertising Derek's number, or failing that, he could ring the vicar. But Derek was still there, working on the vestry roof. He gave Adam a wave when he saw him, and came down the ladder, as if greeting a long lost friend, and for all his general world weariness Adam found it hard not to warm to the man.

They chatted inconsequentially for a few minutes about the lodge until Adam found a natural break in the conversation to bring up the crack in the wall of his garage.

"I'll give my son, Simon, a ring," said Derek, and it was arranged he would come on the Sunday morning. "Mind you, I still cannot fathom to this day why that patio was built there."

"Go on," said Adam, intrigued.

"As you know, David's work took him all over Europe. When the Iron Curtain came down, he spent a year living in Prague, I think, or maybe Budapest. Either way, he let it out to someone he met at Fairhurst Motors..."

"...where he got the Granada from?"

"Yes, David's pride and joy. Anyway, when he came back, he found that patio built right there. He couldn't work out why – but as he said, it was a good place to store flower pots and the like. But it always seemed strange a tenant would do that kind of work."

"Life is full of such mysteries."

"You're right there. Maybe you'll solve it one day. Anyway, I'll get back to the roof, and I see you want to get on. But anything you need before Friday, give me a shout."

"Will do and thank you," said Adam. Little did he know until later just how important this brief exchange had been. But as so often, he was able to remember this exact conversation word for word.

Chapter 7

BROADLEIGH MANOR HOTEL WAS AN unremarkable hotel on the edge of an unremarkable town in the East Midlands. It had once been the seat of a local landowner but was converted in the 1930s at the same time land on either side of the approach road had been sold for squat, unremarkable bungalows. As Sadie walked up the avenue, shortly after meeting Adam for the first time, she realised just how much she hated the place. Her grandfather had bought it in the 1960s and it had remained in the family ever since. Not that she or her older brother Kevin had any intention of carrying on the trade.

Her heart sank when she saw there was yet another new receptionist waiting to greet her. She knew exactly how the conversation would go. "Can I help you?" "No, actually I live here." "I'm sorry, I didn't realise." At least this one had the grace to sound apologetic. Sadie moved on past the bar. As usual at this time of the week it was filled with sales reps, several of whom were conspicuously closing deals on their shiny new phones. At the weekends, these reps would be replaced by American and Japanese tourists visiting the nearby Civil War battlefields and the odd honeymoon couple who couldn't figure out why they had chosen to stay here.

Sadie continued down the side of the kitchen and out onto the path leading to the lodge where her parents lived. Several years previously

Kevin had lined it with an assortment of garden gnomes as a protest against the kitschness of the establishment. Their mother, however, failed to see the irony in his actions and proudly kept them as a souvenir from her little boy. Seeing those gnomes only darkened Sadie's mood. She knew she was about to have a blazing row with her parents, and she wasn't going to win. She had just been chosen for a six-week tour by the university women's cricket team, as the deputy wicket keeper. But her parents were going to insist she worked here over the summer. This would lead Sadie to say how unfair they were being and her mum and dad to remind her who was paying for her education, and so it would go on. Sadie had rehearsed the script by the time she found them in the kitchen, and with a few expletives thrown in, the argument developed exactly as predicted.

That is how in the end Sadie found herself on the Oddballs tour, which only ran for a couple of weeks at the end of June. The Oddballs were a mixed team, in every sense of the word, from university hopefuls to those who thought a packed touring schedule of schools and local clubs sounded like the perfect excuse for a fortnight's partying. There were three women in the team, and Sadie was at least looking forward to showing what she could do against the men.

In reality, Sadie soon found the tour a very different experience from what she was expecting. Em and Kate, it was clear, were only going to be friends with each other, leaving Sadie alone with the boys most evenings. Sadie hated playing their games and pretending to have a good time, and she still resented not being on the university tour. Even though she was playing well, she would gladly have quit, save that she found an ally and companion in Adam. They spent most of their evenings in the corner of the bar, talking about politics or the weather or anything else which particularly interested them. Sadie was grateful that unlike most of his teammates Adam stayed generally sober and didn't try to make a pass at her.

On the field, however, their relationship was considerably more complex. Sadie discovered that keeping wicket to Adam's legbreaks often involved a high degree of guesswork. Usually there were three or four well-pitched balls in an over, but where the other couple landed, if at all, was a complete mystery. But in the end it was Adam's batting that almost destroyed their friendship altogether.

The team had reached the furthest point of their tour, somewhere in a remote corner of Devon. The Oddballs had bowled the locals out fairly cheaply, and Adam's legbreaks had sent three of the batsmen back to the pavilion completely bewildered by their fate. Sadie led the run chase with an energetic half-century but wickets at the other end kept tumbling. By the time Adam came out to bat, she was two short of a maiden century with four runs required. "Just keep your wicket intact," she whispered as the regular number ten took his guard. Adam nodded, and then promptly took a swipe at a wide legside delivery. The ball trickled down to long leg, and should have been an easy single. But long leg for some reason completely missed it and the ball dribbled onto the boundary. The Oddballs had won, and Sadie remained on 98 not out.

Adam offered Sadie his hand, but she just glowered at him and ran off the field where she grudgingly accepted the praise of her teammates. Adam trudged off trying to make sure no-one noticed him. He hadn't meant to spoil Sadie's big moment; it had just been one of those things. But clearly that wasn't how Sadie saw things. While everyone was gathering round her over the post-match tea, she kept throwing dark glances in his direction.

Adam went outside with his cup of tea and found himself engaged by the scorer in a long and seemingly interminable conversation about recording extras. What he hadn't realised was at some point in the afternoon Uncle David had turned up to watch, and by the time he finally broke free and returned to the pavilion, he found Uncle David deep in conversation with Sadie. Uncle David was already fairly crippled by arthritis, but he was lively enough talking about the art of batting. "Talking of which," he said, noticing Adam hovering uncertainly nearby, "here is a master of the art!" At that point, the three of them all burst into laughter and Adam and Sadie's friendship somehow survived their first crisis.

As Sadie drove down to David Pennycome's funeral she found herself still smiling at her only encounter with the old man. He had seemed a kind and generous man then, and whatever exactly her relationship with Adam, she knew he would be glad of her support. So having taken a day off work, she set out early from her home near Birmingham, aiming to arrive at the church in good time. Unfortunately, she was relying on her Satnav which clearly was not familiar with the reality of Devon lanes. After a couple of adventures along narrow holloways with grass growing along their middle, she decided to go where the signposts led her.

It was no real surprise that she slipped in late after the service had already begun. The inside of the church was mercifully cool and peaceful after her adventures, and she took a moment to breathe deeply before taking in the scene before her. At the front was a surprisingly young vicar speaking tenderly about David's life. Sitting directly before him were Adam and his sister Jo. Sadie would recognise Adam's powerful shoulders and severe crew cut anywhere. She didn't know Jo well but from the back she had the same erect bearing as her brother. Behind them scattered around the church were a handful of older people Sadie didn't recognise and on either side of the aisle a small military guard of honour.

Sadie had been to the funeral of a couple of elderly relatives before and this service followed exactly the same format: a couple of hymns, a sermon, a few prayers. The only surprise was the Austrian folk tune which seemed oddly out of place with the military recession out of the church. As Sadie stood to pay her respects her eyes met Adam's. He was following the coffin, with Jo leaning on his arm. His deep, dark eyes briefly brightened while Jo looked at her more suspiciously, with a fleeting, nervous expression that didn't betray her eye colour. They all met outside in the shade of a yew tree where Sadie agreed to go with them to a local woodland burial ground David had already chosen in his will.

As the coffin was lowered into the ground, Sadie decided she really didn't like funerals. Her philosophy had always been to look forward, to seek new opportunities, and explore new possibilities. The pile of earth by the grave challenged that philosophy, and Sadie didn't like to be challenged. She stepped to one side as the young vicar pronounced a closing blessing and Adam and Jo each threw in a rose. What meaning lay in that ritual she wasn't sure, and she wasn't planning to find out any time soon. Still Adam seemed glad she had come, and she found herself offering the usual platitudes.

However, Sadie excused herself from the wake, on the pretext she wouldn't know anyone. "See you later," said Adam, handing her the key, and she gave him a peck on the cheek. "Bedroom at the back of the house," added Jo, in a flat, neutral tone. Sadie thanked her and set off back to the lodge. It had been a hard week, and she was glad of a brief moment to herself.

The lodge was a solid, Victorian brick building almost lost behind a laurel hedge. Weeds peeped through the gravel on the drive, and the straggling woody shrubs that stood by either side of the door hinted at recent neglect. Sadie suspected this was a place that urgently needed an infusion of life and colour, and her suspicions were only confirmed when she opened the front door. The whole house was painted in dark, heavy colours with shabby, but comfortable, furniture to match. Sadie wondered if Adam had even noticed. She went upstairs to her bedroom, and found walls painted a strange shade of olive green and a faded patterned carpet stained in a couple of places. Adam had at least provided new bed linen, although the abstract black and white pattern of the duvet cover betrayed his stubbornly bachelor ways. At the very least the room needed some fresh flowers even though Sadie doubted there was a vase to be found anywhere. She drew back the fawn curtains and saw an overgrown garden in desperate need of attention, and at that moment decided that although she knew little about gardening, here was her project for the weekend.

Sadie was a great believer in getting things done, and she welcomed a challenge. But first there was that cashflow forecast to complete. She lost herself for a couple of hours in her spreadsheet before Adam and Jo returned. Her online business was rapidly growing but funding was proving a constant struggle. At least once it was done she could enjoy a weekend off, and she knew Adam and Jo would provide the company she secretly admitted only to herself she needed.

To her relief Adam and Jo welcomed the idea of tackling the garden. The three of them were gathered in the study, now free of its hospital bed, and surrounded by piles of old books, they talked late into the evening, catching up with each other. Adam and Jo shared what little they had found out about Uncle David from the reception, that everyone knew him as a shy, but friendly, member of the local community, interested in bird-watching and history, who faithfully served his country and loved travelling round Europe. Even so, as Sadie listened, she got the impression they still didn't know who he really was. Eventually the conversation turned, and soon Adam and

Sadie were deep in discussion about the new England cricket captain. Sadie noticed Jo didn't say much, but followed their toing and froing with keen and oddly penetrating sharp grey eyes. Her mood lightened when Sadie brought some samples from her product range. They shared a simple supper of wholewheat crackers, hummus and pitted olives, washed down with goji juice. Then Jo announced she was going to bed, and Sadie followed suit.

Adam gave them both a hug, and then sat for a while, deliberating. Every time Sadie breezed into his life, he found himself rehearsing the history of their relationship. That rather shambolic cricket tour had somehow strengthened their bond and in the following months their friendship had followed the same pattern of intense times together, with brief and not so brief interludes in between. Some weeks they would spend long evenings together, vehemently debating the latest hot issues and generally depleting Adam's supply of best filter coffee. Some weeks they barely shared a word, as other concerns and friendships pressed in. But one way or another they always seemed to find each other, knowing that the one would always be there for the other.

The only topic they never discussed was their own relationship which remained undefined until the night of Leon's party. Leon was the current captain of the Oddballs, and he was renowned for his boozy parties which frequently attracted the attention of the university authorities. Adam and Sadie arrived late and stayed only until Leon and his merry band started drinking shots. They retreated to Adam's flat where he put on the coffee machine and they began another of their discussions covering topics from haircuts to education, dance music to of course cricket. Sadie was seated on Adam's bed, as usual, her legs tucked under her, wearing her familiar pair of black leggings and a floral top. Before they knew it, it was midnight. Usually Sadie would finish the last of her coffee, give Adam a quick kiss and then take her leave. But tonight somehow it was different. Sadie came over to Adam and kissed him full on the lips. Adam looked at her in surprise, and she looked back. Then Adam kissed her back and soon they were in each other's arms, and what Adam had been half hoping for, half fearing came to pass.

The next morning Sadie was gone. As Adam woke up, the scent of her skin still lay heavy on the sheet, and he found a few of her hairs on the pillow. But Sadie herself was not there. Adam replayed the events of the previous night, and tried to make sense of what happened. Their lovemaking had seemed so special and so joyful, and yet Sadie's absence troubled him. He tried to contact her but there was no reply. He left several messages, but it seemed as if she had gone to ground. He thought about going round to her flat but wondered what he would say if her flatmates were there.

In the end he wandered down to the nets where he had first met her. She was practising keeping wicket, and he observed her unnoticed while she took catches behind the stumps. He noticed for the first time the grace and beauty of her movement as she twisted first this way and then that. Eventually the session came to an end and as she took off her helmet, she passed her hand through her hair in that special way of hers. Then she caught sight of Adam and waved – partly, Adam suspected for the benefit of onlookers.

Sadie came up to him. "We need to talk," said Adam.

"We do," said Sadie, "give me ten minutes to change, and then let's find somewhere no-one can hear us."

Behind the cricket ground ran a rather grubby urban canal. Adam and Sadie walked along banks, past graffiti-scarred factories, through a rundown estate, alongside rather more desirable waterside properties until they finally reached the fringe of the countryside. All the while they moved forward in silence, hand in hand, trying not to look at the other.

When they found a bench which was clean enough to sit on, they sat and turned to each other. Adam put his hand on Sadie's thigh, and she held it tightly there. Eventually she spoke, and to this day Adam still remembered the conversation.

"You know I've often talked about travelling and seeing the world?"

"Er, yes..."

"Yesterday I had an email from a family friend. He owns a hotel in Melbourne, and he offered me a job as a manager there."

"As I remember, you didn't say anything about that last night."

"I wanted to tell you, I really did. But I wasn't quite sure how to say it."

"How about, 'I've just been offered a job in Melbourne'?"

"Don't be mean. It wasn't as simple as that."

"Why not?"

"Because as we sat talking, part of me kept thinking how I didn't want to say goodbye. And then midnight came, and I thought about leaving, and I found I couldn't. Not last night, anyway."

"But you left this morning."

"Oh, I know I am going to take the job," said Sadie looking straight at Adam with those piercing green eyes, "but I want you to know one day I will come back. For you. That is, if you will wait for me."

Adam was silent for a while. What indeed could he say? On the one hand, he had found a woman who seemed to genuinely care for him. On the other, it seemed as if he was being bound by a commitment he wasn't that sure he was willing to make.

"At least you're not gone yet. Let's make the most of what we have."

"Agreed," replied Sadie. They were about to kiss when a large wet dog bound up to them, followed by an old man swearing loudly at his not so faithful friend.

Adam and Sadie spent the next few weeks in an intimate but chaste friendship. They decided to concentrate on the forthcoming exams, although Adam quickly learnt Sadie had a very different understanding of concentration. She could spend hours staring at a screen or writing notes, only pausing from time to time to do some stretching exercises, or to make a cup of strong coffee. Adam for his part found himself more often studying her rather than revising a subject that had long ceased to excite him, and counted down the days to when the books could be put away.

In the end finals came. It was no surprise Sadie got a first; it was rather more of a shock to Adam to discover he had somehow scraped an upper second. At least he had reason to tell his parents that three years at university had not been wasted, even though their congratulations over the phone sounded half-hearted at best.

Adam and Sadie celebrated these results by going together on their last ever Oddballs tour. Most of the time was spent travelling or dossing down on hall floors, so there was little opportunity for them to be alone. However, for the last match Leon found somewhere the funds to take over the entire wing of a small country hotel, nestled in rolling countryside somewhere in the heart of England, and the team's arrival there coincided with Sadie receiving her work permit. So she went out and finally scored the century she had long deserved. Adam was down the other end at the time, and he gave her a big hug in the middle of the pitch. Then, although he wasn't known for his batting prowess, they forged an unbeaten partnership that in the end proved too much for the opposition, who like most of the other teams were mystified by his random assortment of legbreaks.

After the match came the inevitable team dinner. This was the first time Adam saw Sadie in a dress, a low cut cotton number that perfectly matched the colour of her eyes. They sat together through the meal and the first couple of speeches, but as the evening started to become rowdier, she slipped her hand in his, and said, "Shall we go for a walk?"

Outside the hotel the sun was starting to set over tranquil fields where horses grazed peacefully, and sheep stood stock-still as they contemplated the couple walking by. Adam and Sadie were talking about everything, and nothing in particular, as if fearing to join in with the silence. They had no clear idea where they were going, but the lane led them on, up a gentle rise and through a belt of trees until suddenly the landscape ahead of them fell away, and they found themselves looking across a broad river valley with hazy, golden hills beyond.

They stopped, awestruck by the view, and their conversation halted. Eventually Sadie gently laid her hand on his arm and asked, "Are you going to be all right?" Adam shrugged his shoulders, and took her hand. They walked back to the hotel slowly and thoughtfully, and sooner than they realised they were standing outside listening to the singing and laughter from the dinner.

"Do you think we should join them?" asked Adam.

At that moment, the star opening batsman rushed out of the front door and threw up in the flowerbed.

"I think we have our answer," laughed Sadie. Then she led him up into her bedroom where without a second thought they began to make love. Neither said very much from that point; they were in a twilight world where their hopes could not be put into words, where there were too many questions without answers. All they could do was give themselves to each other until in the growing darkness they became one flesh, and finally in the depths of the night they fell asleep in each other's arms, deeply, deeply satisfied.

Chapter 8

ADAM NEVER FORGOT HOW THE next few months were the most miserable of his life. Sadie was gone and although she regularly sent messages and pictures, he yearned for her presence. But yearning was not going to provide Adam with an income. So with a heavy heart he decided to train as a teacher, not out of any sense of vocation but simply because he did not know what else to do with a degree in politics, and hell would freeze over before he became a politician.

However, it turned out Adam had some ability as a teacher, and he found young people generally responded well to his clear and thorough explanations of any given topic. The trouble was, teaching could only ever be a job for him, and yet he quickly realised it was a profession that demanded his whole life. But in the absence of any alternative, he plodded through the modules and assignments in the same way he had plodded through his degree, and passed each one through his detailed, methodological approach.

As part of his training, he ended up on placement at a down at heels comprehensive that had tried and failed to reinvent itself as a cutting edge, go-ahead academy. Most of his contact time seemed to involve peacemaking and reconciliation work among groups of particularly disaffected teenagers. Usually his efforts bore some fruit; even so, there were two students in year 10, called Charlie and Bobby, who for some reason hated each other with a passion, and they defied all attempts to negotiate a truce, no matter how much staff tried to negotiate a settlement.

It was an unseasonably warm spring day just before the Easter holidays. Adam had had Charlie and Bobby in the last class of the day, and he breathed a sigh of relief when the bell went. He stayed on for a while to do some marking in the relative silence of the classroom and then he went for his bus. He had almost reached the bus stop when he heard the sound of groaning from an alleyway. It was Bobby; he had been stabbed in the thigh and was losing a lot of blood.

Adam rushed to him, and, without thinking, made a tourniquet from his belt in an effort to stem the wound. As he phoned for an ambulance, other students began to gather. Some were crying and hugging each other; others were laughing and taking photos. All the time Adam tried to keep Bobby awake until the ambulance arrived, and he could finally hand him over to the paramedics.

By now the police had arrived and taped off the area as a crime scene. In all the general confusion Adam stood and watched as they carried out their work. A couple were keeping bystanders at bay, and taking down names and addresses. Others were busy securing evidence, while another sat down with him, asked a few brief questions and arranged for Adam to be interviewed as a witness later on. It was only later that the reality of what had happened sank in, as back at the school he changed out of his bloody clothes, and found himself retching in the cloakroom sink.

But by then Adam knew he had found his vocation. He spent the rest of the school year preparing for his application to the police force, which to his immense relief was accepted. There was just one downside; in order to start training, he would have to cancel his planned trip to Australia, to see Sadie. Yet she seemed to understand,

and to share in his happiness, and they continued to exchange news and photos regularly. It was good to see Sadie looking so healthy and happy, and her warm smile kept Adam going through training and on into those early months of probation, where, despite his lowly rank, he quickly forged his reputation for being a hardworking, honest, team player, who was willing to learn and not afraid to admit his shortcomings.

Yet in the middle of a dank, sodden February contact suddenly stopped. Adam was about to pursue an opening in the Serious Crimes Unit, and he wanted to tell Sadie the news. But for the next few days there was no reply, no response. Adam anxiously scanned previous communications for any sign something was amiss, or some coolness in their relationship. However, despite his many fears, he found nothing. Sadie was enjoying the outdoor life of an Australian summer, and working hard with her newfound Korean friends, Grace and Ruby. So why the silence? Adam spent sleepless nights and despite his rapidly developing skills in detection could find no satisfactory answer.

Eventually, after about a week, Adam received a message from a previously unknown number: *Hello, this is Sadie. I can't explain everything that is going on. I am safe, I will be in touch again when I can, but that may be some time. Please take care of yourself and know that I love you very much.* Adam wanted to reply instantly, but not knowing whose phone was being used, thought better of it. Instead he spent the next couple of hours reading and re-reading the message. It seemed that Sadie was in some kind of danger, but what precisely he could not tell. He thought about alerting the authorities in Melbourne but decided it was probably an overreaction.

So Adam waited and waited. Days turned into weeks; weeks into months. Sometimes he would go back through all their messages and think about happier times. Sometimes he would try to live as if his relationship with Sadie had never happened, and aim to live looking forward. Yet somehow he could not free himself – so instead he plunged ever more deeply into his work. From time to time colleagues attempted to quiz him about his private life, but he simply ignored them, and all the rumours that some spread about this quiet, dedicated rookie who seemed to be always on the case.

Eventually Adam did strike up one particular friendship, with the newly arrived PC Blessing McQueen. Her father Victor had been an opposition leader in Zimbabwe and was now driving buses in Stratford. Blessing seemed impressed that Adam knew something about the political situation there; he was merely grateful that for once his degree had come in useful. And there was another connection as well. Blessing's brother Wesley had once played cricket for Zimbabwe under-19s and he played for a club Adam knew well, even though Adam suspected he would hit most of his legbreaks for six.

They started to meet up when they could for lunch in the canteen and to exchange messages, even though at first such exchanges left Adam feeling very uneasy. They tried to work out when they could start seeing each other more regularly, but with changing shifts and the perennial shortage of staff it took a very long time before they could make a definite date.

That evening Adam left work early for once. There was a sense of joy he hadn't felt for a long time, and the burden he felt about his current case didn't seem quite as heavy. He took time to get himself ready, but even so he realised he would still be arriving far too early. So he checked his messages, and to his surprise there was one from Sadie: *I know it's been nearly a year, but I think I am free again to start talking, if you want. I don't want to talk about what has happened – you need only know that finally my stalker has left me alone and I am slowly starting to rebuild my life. You may have moved on, and I would understand, but I would like to hear from you, just to know you are well and safe. I have been praying so much for you.*

Adam sat on the edge of his bed while a cold breeze whipped against his window. He read and reread the message. There were so many questions. Why hadn't Sadie told him she had been stalked? Was she really safe? And what was this about praying? That certainly wasn't the Sadie he had known. Sitting there with his many thoughts, he suddenly realised that time was slipping by, and Blessing would be expecting him.

They had settled on a Caribbean restaurant on the South Bank. Blessing had arrived several minutes before him, but she only responded to his apology with a broad, open smile Adam found irresistible. She was wearing a yellow dress with earrings and necklace to match, and tight black leggings, which emphasised the shape of her sleek, athletic body. As they began their meal, Adam realised he had never noticed before the way she gracefully turned her fingers as she spoke, or the bright laughter that punctuated her conversation. Yet even so, as he enjoyed the physical pleasure of the moment, he realised he was watching far more than engaging, and that part of him was far, far away in another time, another place.

Towards the end of the meal, however, Adam suddenly became aware Blessing had asked him a question and was waiting for a reply. She was looking at him with questioning, serious eyes and Adam wished he had been paying more attention.

"So why did you become a policeman, Adam?"

Adam hesitated. He had spent many a night dreaming about Bobby, the blood soaking through his trousers, the confident, cocky teenager once again a frightened schoolboy crying out for his mother. Sometimes in his dreams the paramedics arrived in time; sometimes they did not, and he could feel the weight of Bobby's head cold and clammy in his lap, before waking up in a cold sweat and inching back to reality through the thick darkness all around him.

"You don't have to talk about it," she said kindly, resting her hand on his arm.

"I saved someone's life and I saw how the police responded. But I don't want to talk about it. Not now." In fact Adam had never shared with anyone anything more than the information he had put down in his statement. Yet in that instant he knew that one day he would have to tell the whole story. Only it would not be to Blessing. It would be to Sadie.

Gently he withdrew his arm, and asked for the bill. Once it was paid, they walked close together under Adam's umbrella until they reached the tube station, where Blessing gave Adam a hug and drew him close to herself. "Take me home," Blessing whispered, and Adam could feel himself responding physically. But as Blessing spoke, he could somehow hear Sadie's voice on the last night of the cricket tour.

"Sadly, not tonight," he replied, "there's something I need to do."

"I don't make this offer very often," said Blessing.

"I know," said Adam as he released her.

She gave him a quick peck on the cheek and then disappeared into the crowds, with Adam watching on.

On the journey home Adam wondered why he felt such a strong bond with Sadie. He had grown up with the notion sex was just another bodily function. You had sex with whoever you wanted whenever you wanted, providing the other person was of age and had given their consent. Yet he realised this notion was a lie. Sex – certainly when it came to Sadie – created a deep personal bond that persisted in spite of the distance between them, and even though it had been nearly a year since they had last spoken, he could not deny the reality of the bond they had forged together.

That didn't make the evening any easier. As he got off the tube, he was tempted to ring Blessing and tell her that he had changed his mind, or that he had finished his task sooner than expected. He doubted that she would come over, but there was always a chance. Yet there was this little voice deep inside him that stopped him making that call. Where that came from, or why it was so adamant, he couldn't rightly say. But it was there, and it could not be ignored.

Adam slowly, thoughtfully unlocked the door of the flat and switched on the light. He headed over to his laptop and spilt out his frustration and anger in a long, bitter email that he promptly deleted. Then he started again and wrote a polite, friendly response assuring Sadie that he was still there and was waiting for her.

As it turned out, the opportunity to see Sadie came far sooner than he expected. In the late summer, when the city was slumbering under a dry, smoky haze, Adam received a brief message to say that her father had suffered a near fatal heart attack, and she was coming home for good. Over the next few weeks he received regular updates, and encouragements to pray, which he wasn't quite sure how to respond to. He did try to pray on a few occasions, and whether it was his stumbling words, or the quality of medical care, somehow Sadie's father gradually improved.

And then in the middle of October, just as the first chill winds were whipping up the Thames, Sadie said she was coming down to London on business, and could they meet up for a quick lunch? At that time Adam was in the middle of the case that would eventually earn him his promotion, and DS Spencer was certainly surprised when Adam actually asked for a couple of hours' downtime. He trusted Adam enough, however, not to ask for an explanation, and as it turned out, DC Sawyer guessed the reason at the first attempt. "Don't rush back," he grinned.

There was a reasonable Chinese buffet close to the police station, and Adam excused himself early to make sure he was there first. When about ten minutes had passed, he began to worry Sadie wouldn't show, even though he had never known her to miss an appointment. But suddenly she was there, and Adam almost leapt out of his seat to greet her.

Sadie had gone through university generally wearing hoodies and trainers, and with short, tousled hair she regularly had to smooth back into place. But as she entered, Adam noticed the transformation. Her hair was longer now, carefully tied back into a long ponytail she had pinned up into a bun. She was wearing a white linen blouse and long black skirt, with a simple silver cross around her neck, and what looked like a charm bracelet on her wrist.

"You look stunning," said Adam, as he gave her a quick kiss.

"Good afternoon to you," said Sadie, laughing. "Sorry I'm late, my meeting overran."

They helped themselves to the buffet, and then searched for the quietest corner for a conversation.

"So what brings you to London?" asked Adam.

"Well, you are here, so I suppose that's an attraction," said Sadie.

"I guess it is."

"But seriously – you remember my schoolfriend Morwenna I told you about? She wanted me to run an online operation for her foodie business. I said I would run a standalone entity with her products, but also stock it with various world foods. So here I am, meeting with potential investors, discussing cashflow, profit forecasts and all the stuff you really want me to talk about."

Adam smiled. "You seem happy."

"I've had my moments over the past few years. And I guess I'm relieved my father's still here, even if he will never quite be the same again. But looking forward, yes, I think I am happy, and glad to be home. What about you?"

"Do you remember those evenings when we would talk endlessly about what we wanted to do with our lives...?"

"And never really reached a conclusion...?"

"Yes, those evenings. I think I have found at last what I want to do."

"I'm glad."

The conversation paused as they tucked into their food, both aware that there was so much they wanted to say, but not sure how to fit it all into this all too brief space.

Finally Adam asked Sadie about the cross around her neck.

"Ah, that's a keepsake. I think I have told you about my friends Grace and Ruby? They were the ones who protected me when I was being stalked, and made sure I was never on my own. Grace's mother ran a Korean restaurant, and Ruby's father pastored the local Korean church. So one way or another, I spent a lot of time surrounded by food or in meetings. And even when I was in my flat, sometimes one or both of them would sleep over with me, to make sure I was OK."

"They sound like very special friends."

"They are – I think you would like to meet them some time. They spent a lot of time talking with me, reading the Bible, answering my questions. They gave me this cross when I was baptised, just before I had to come home."

"You were baptised?"

"I could tell you the whole story, but that's probably for another time. For now, I reckon it's time for desserts."

They continued chatting for a while until Adam suddenly realised he was due back at the station.

"Sorry, big case on."

"No need to apologise," said Sadie. "You seem, if not happy, then certainly content with what you are doing."

"It can be nasty work at times, but yes, I am content."

Sadie laid her hand on his arm, and Adam thought how Blessing had made the exact same gesture. But this time he let the hand rest.

"Can I see you later?"

"No, I've got to get back," said Sadie, "and besides, we need some time to get to know each other again, don't we?"

Adam thought about the woman who had walked into the restaurant a couple of hours before and he knew in his heart that she was right. Somehow in all his years of waiting, he had imagined that Sadie would still be the same, but now he realised that was a foolish notion. He was different, so was she, and both of them in their own way had grown up. Even so, as he saw Sadie put on her long woollen coat, and carefully flick out her ponytail, he knew the bond between them would from that point on only grow stronger.

As Adam went to bed that night, he reflected that it had been nearly a year since that meeting. They had communicated regularly since then, and he counted her a genuine friend. Yet they had seen each other only intermittently and fleetingly, and he wanted, no needed, some permanence in their relationship. Maybe at the end of the weekend they would have a chance to talk, to decide together what kind of future they wanted. Certainly from his perspective that conversation was long overdue. Yet the main thing was, Sadie was here, under his roof, and he would have two more days with her. Comforted by that thought, he finally went to sleep, no longer dreading the darkness all about him, until in the early morning the smell of breakfast woke him.

Chapter 9

THE NEXT MORNING SADIE WOKE up while it was still dark. She glanced at her phone and realised it was exactly the same time she had woken up on the last morning of the cricket tour. She remembered how then she had prised herself from Adam's arms to go to the toilet, and then attempted to settle back as quietly as possible in his embrace. But as she settled once again on his strong, muscular chest, he instinctively held her once again, without breaking his slumber, and Sadie settled to go back to sleep.

But the sleep just would not come. Her mind was by now fully awake. She was thinking of her forthcoming departure to Australia and the many practical details that needed sorting. She was thinking of Adam and all the time they had spent together. She was thinking about the present and all that had happened last night, and try as she might, she could not bring any order to her many jumbled and confusing thoughts. So she lay, listening to Adam's slow, relaxed breathing, trying to remain as still as possible, and yet growing ever more conscious of her disquiet.

At one point Sadie wondered if she should try praying, but then she reasoned God would hardly listen to her, naked and lying in her boyfriend's arms. She was then just about to break free, when she became aware of the sound of a bird starting to sing with a loud and clear song. Although she knew little about nature, she reckoned it was a blackbird. Soon there were other songs as well, each new melody interweaving with the other, and for the first time in her life Sadie heard the beauty and the wonder of dawn chorus.

In a little while the darkness gave way to a greyer light, that slowly, slowly grew stronger. Adam's breathing became shallower, and he began to run his hand up and down her back, and kiss her hair. And for all her confusion Sadie could feel herself responding physically to his touch. She rolled over and before long succumbed to the sheer pleasure of the moment.

Since then, Sadie often wondered what would have happened if she had even at that late stage pulled out of her work commitment. But she had come to a fork in the road, and had chosen her route, and she reasoned it was futile wondering what would have happened if she had made another choice. She also knew that another fork in the road was coming up fast in front of her, and although the decision was in theory simple, her experience with Tucker Magee had considerably complicated matters.

As the dawn chorus started on this new morning in a new and unfamiliar place, Sadie decided it was no use trying to get back to sleep again. She needed to fill her mind with other thoughts, with other perspectives. So as she listened to the birdsong, she did some vigorous warming up exercises while meditating on a verse from her Bible app. Then even though it was still early, she had a shower, got dressed and cooked breakfast.

Sadie hoped Adam would be the first one up, but instead it was Jo who emerged first. She tried hard to hide her disappointment, and sought to engage Adam's sister in conversation, so that by the time Adam joined them, they had already formed a plan for the garden. In essence, any plant they did not recognise would have to go.

Breakfast done, Sadie slipped out to the garden centre to get some tools and some gloves while Adam and Jo tidied up.

"She's quite a force to be reckoned with," remarked Jo as they washed the plates.

"She is that," said Adam.

"So?"

"What do you mean, so?" asked Adam.

At this point Jo once again retreated to her usual shy embarrassed self and refused to say any more. But Adam knew exactly what Jo was asking. He only wished he had an answer.

Jo watched on as Adam and Sadie started on the bindweed, brambles and nettles in front of the conservatory. It was harder work than they had expected, and the roots went far deeper than they had imagined. Yet for all that, Jo couldn't help noticing how well they worked together, and they talked about every little detail. From time to time they came over to her, as she bagged up the plants, or she brought them drinks, and despite the slow progress, Jo saw that bit by bit they were gradually and systematically bringing order to the wilderness.

By lunchtime, there was at least a view from the lounge, even if the ramshackle shed at the far end of the garden still remained an unattainable goal. Jo was happy to slip inside and make a picnic, while Adam described his plans to lay down a new path across the garden, and Sadie gently teased him about his obsession to detail.

They were just on the point of finishing lunch, when the classic car restorer arrived to pick up the Granada estate. It was, of course, a non-starter. Adam and the man called Freddie gently eased it out of its slumbers and onto the lowloader.

"This might take a few months," said Freddie, "but I guess you're not in any rush?"

Adam shook his head. "Just glad to find someone to take it on. From what I understand it was my great-uncle's pride and joy."

"It will be a pleasure working on it," said Freddie, as he completed the paperwork.

As he carefully exited, Simon turned up to look at the patio. "I'll come back tomorrow to do the bulk of the work," he explained, "but I just wanted to see the issue for myself." He and Adam then disappeared into the garage while Jo and Sadie went back to work on the garden. "You and Adam make a great team," said Jo, as they tackled the laurel hedge.

"That comes from keeping wicket to him," laughed Sadie, "you have to learn to expect the unexpected."

At that point Adam returned. "Our first visitors," he said proudly, "might get used to this." He took up the clippers, with the result that he and Sadie resumed their partnership, leaving Jo feeling rather redundant. At that precise point she couldn't help feeling resentful how tomorrow she would be returning to her cramped room, travelling each day to a job she didn't particularly enjoy and then coming home to noisy neighbours arguing or having sex, or sometimes doing both at the same time. But then she had always felt one way or another invisible, even to her own family, and while Adam did his best to look after her, she fully appreciated he had his own life to lead. So she went back to bagging up and making the drinks until everyone decided one way or another they needed a break. It was a hot afternoon, and while the patch of trees beyond the far hedge created a little shade, they preferred to seek sanctuary in the cool of the living room and check out the day's football.

A little later that evening Jo wanted to retire early, but Adam insisted she stayed. Whether it was because he wanted time with his sister, or felt awkward being on his own with Sadie, Jo couldn't say.

But Sadie had found a collection of board games at the back of the dining room sideboard, and for a few hours over pizza and drinks everyone unwound and let the deeper questions sink to the back of their minds.

Whose idea it was to go to church next morning, no-one could rightly say. Jo certainly was surprised when Adam brought up the topic. Neither of them had ever had many dealings with church growing up, and religion was the one thing Adam never discussed. Yet she could sense that somehow going there was important to him. Sadie too seemed keen, and Jo realised that the cross around her neck was more than just another piece of jewellery. As for her, she was happy enough to tag along, and do what everyone was doing. After all, she reasoned no harm could come of it, and it would at most be only an hour.

That is how on the Sunday Adam walked hand in hand with Sadie along to St Alban's, chatting about nothing in particular, with Jo lagging behind, wondering what to expect. She had worried she hadn't brought anything formal to wear, even if Adam had assured her that there was no particular dress code, and she was concerned she would stick out like the proverbial sore thumb.

Jo needn't have worried, however. Even though James the vicar was leading a service elsewhere, Derek welcomed them all with his usual friendly smile, and once the faithful few sensed her discomfort, they instead focused their attention on Adam and Sadie, who to all impressions seemed the perfect couple. And so, gradually relaxing, Jo actually found she started to enjoy the service, even if there were words she struggled to understand, and remained confused throughout when to stand or sit or kneel.

The final hymn was just finishing, however, when Adam's phone began to vibrate. Jo glanced at Adam who seemed uncertain whether to answer it. "It's Simon," he whispered. "He wants us to come back at once."

"Then we better go," said Sadie, who as soon as the blessing was pronounced slipped out of the pew.

Simon was already halfway down the lane by the time they exited the church. He seemed visibly shaken, and reluctant to speak, running his hand nervously through his jet black hair. Refusing to answer any questions, he led them in silence back through the house, and to the ground he had excavated under the patio, where he stopped and pointed wordlessly. But the gesture was unnecessary. For it was plain to everyone that there amid the roots of the sapling were unmistakably the fragments of a human skull, and a dark secret that had just been unearthed.

Chapter 10

SADIE ALWAYS REMEMBERED HOW IN that instant Adam immediately switched into professional mode. Without any trace of emotion, he turned to the rest of them and said, "OK, what we have here may or may not be a crime scene. You will all be asked to provide a statement and then you will be free to leave. Jo and Sadie, I suggest you pack up and go at this point."

"I can take Jo as far as Reading."

"Thank you, that would be great."

"Will you be all right?" asked Jo.

"Don't worry about me. This is my natural environment, after all. Not quite sure what this will do to the probate value, though," added Adam with a note of black humour.

"Anything I can do?" asked Simon, who was still visibly trembling.

"Not really – just leave everything exactly as you found it. But do ring your father. There's something he told me the other day he needs to tell the police. He will remember the conversation. And this is important for all of you, don't go spreading this story around. The last thing the team at Peninsula needs is a news story about a retired policeman with a body buried in his garden. Not good for business, as they say." With that Adam dialled 999 and reported the discovery of human remains.

It took half an hour for the first police officer to turn up. In the meanwhile Jo made a cup of tea and booked her train ticket. Sadie sorted out the fridge and then both women started packing in stunned silence. Adam helped Simon pack up his tools, and they stood making awkward small talk until a fresh faced young constable called PC Timms turned up.

"Report of human remains?" he said cheerfully as if this was some kind of joke.

Adam produced his warrant card. "Report of human remains," he echoed grimly.

"There's a detective coming up from Drumchester," said the constable apologetically, "but I guess we might need a full team."

"I guess," said Adam forcefully.

A couple of hours later several police cars and a van had descended on Little Netherworthy Lodge. Jo and Sadie made their statements, loaded up their bags and left. They journeyed onto the motorway saying very little. Sadie sensed that even in more normal circumstances Jo would have been a shy, nervous passenger. She found company in a one-day international on the radio, where the familiar voices of the TMS team and the routine of the game enabled her to find at least some kind of escape.

Mercifully, the journey to Reading was without major incident. As they turned into the station car park, Sadie turned to Jo with her stock question: "Are you going to be all right?" Jo shrugged her shoulders. "Depends if the neighbours let me sleep. But there's nothing a stiff drink won't cure."

Sadie parked up and helped Jo get her bag out the boot. Just as Jo was about to leave, she gave Sadie a gentle kiss and added, "You know Adam loves you very much."

Sadie nodded.

"Don't keep him waiting forever." Then, fearing she had spoken out of turn, she mumbled, "Thank you for the lift," and made as if to walk away.

"Hey," said Sadie, lightly touching her shoulder, "shall we meet up again soon?"

Jo turned round, clearly startled by the positive response, and for a moment Sadie saw a genuine smile on her face.

"Give me a ring," Jo said, "I would very much like that." And with a little wave she disappeared into the masses all heading for their own particular destinations.

As for Sadie, once she had managed to navigate her way out of Reading, the remaining journey was mercifully brief. She was still struggling to come to terms with the awful discovery of the morning, and for the first time in a good few years she suddenly felt very much on her own. She walked slowly and thoughtfully up to her flat and as she opened the door she was struck by the silence inside. She put on some music, and thought about what to do next. She hadn't eaten since breakfast, but she couldn't face food – at least not yet. She loaded the washing machine, put out the rubbish, doing whatever chore she could find to distract her mind. And then she decided to ring Adam.

Adam had just arrived back home when the call came through. He had spent a good couple of hours making his acquaintance with DI Gregory of the Peninsula Serious Crimes Unit and even though Adam was the subject of the interrogation, he had instantly warmed to the man. DI Gregory clearly had a quick mind and was used to asking decisive questions, and Adam suspected he was used to getting results. So Adam set out as clearly as he could how his Great-Uncle David had left him the property and how he was awaiting probate.

"So you have no idea why he left you this house?"

Adam shook his head.

"And your great-uncle lived in this house for thirty-two years?"

"I understand that early on he let it out for a few months at a time while working round Europe."

"We will talk to the solicitor tomorrow. You say his name is Christopher Brunt?"

Adam nodded. "There is some paperwork in the boxes for the tip in the garage. There may be something in there. And you can speak to the gentleman I mentioned called Derek. He seems to know far more about his house than anyone else."

"We are taking his statement as we speak. Right then," and here DI Gregory rose from the faded armchair in the lounge, "I think we are done for now. I know where I can find you. You know the drill – no press, no social media, and no private investigation." He cracked a slight smile in his thin, careworn face, and stretched his taut, sinewy calves. He was, Adam decided, clearly someone who had run a few marathons and who brought as much discipline to his body as to his investigation.

"Understood. But I will need to tell my superior officer in the morning."

"They'll be delighted, I'm sure."

DI Gregory extended his hand if not in friendship, then in recognition of a common cause, and in that split second the two men weighed up the strength of each other's grip. Then Adam handed over the keys, and left just as yet more investigators in white suits entered the crime scene – if indeed the house was a crime scene.

"Hello, it's been a day hasn't it?" said Sadie.

"Yep," said Adam, putting down his bag.

"How are you holding up?"

Adam paused. What could he say? Throughout the journey home he had been piecing together his memories of Uncle David's life. He had always known Uncle David to be a model of kindness and consideration, but he realised that he had but a very few fragments of a life that was far richer, and far more complex than he had imagined. And from a professional point of view, he knew from experience that even the kindest and most considerate person could, under certain circumstances, commit the greatest evil. Yet was Uncle David such a person? The conversation with Derek gave him some reassurance, yet he also knew from experience memories could be faulty – if indeed Derek was telling the truth. It could always be instead that Derek was the killer, or was working together with David. But that, he told himself, was absurd – wasn't it?

"Physically, I'm fine. But there's a lot to process. I hope the officers interviewing you weren't too hard on you."

"Oh, that was fine. It was just routine, as far as I can tell."

For a moment, an awkward silence followed. There was good reason why Adam and Sadie rarely spoke over the phone – messages didn't allow for spaces, and for embarrassing pauses.

"So look," said Sadie eventually, "with all that happened, we didn't get to talk, did we?"

"No, we didn't," said Adam emphatically.

"When can we next see each other?"

Adam smiled. Usually when Sadie saw him, she just announced she was turning up.

"I'm afraid it may not be for a while. I am going back to a major surveillance op tomorrow. It may take weeks, if not months."

"But when you're free – contact me, please."

Adam picked up Sadie's tone immediately. "Of course," he said warmly, "and I will keep in touch as much as I can. Love you."

"Love you too."

Sadie breathed deeply when the call ended, and unexpectedly found that she was crying. She turned on the music again, and blowing her nose, she checked her messages. Most were from suppliers and usually she would have spent the rest of the evening replying. But tonight, she decided they could wait. One of her messages, however, was from her former boyfriend Damien. He lived not too far away, but as Sadie knew all too well, only got in touch when there was something he wanted.

Hi Sadie. This is a bit of a weird one. So I have this client and like he's suddenly started talking about Christian stuff. He keeps inviting me along to a course – there's free food involved, apparently – but I keep putting him off. Are you able to come with me on Thursday evening? It would be great if you could come with.

Sadie smiled. She could do with some form of distraction, even if her feelings for Damien had died years ago. So she arranged to pick him up just before seven – making sure, as always, that strict boundaries were in place. Even as she typed, however, she wondered when exactly she and Adam would meet up and whether she would have the courage to tell him all she needed to say. At least she was going to see Jo soon, and maybe that would help. She made a mental note to ring her in the next couple of days and then, as was her custom, phoned home.

"Is everything all right?" asked her father.

"Why do you ask?"

"You don't sound your usual self."

Sadie realised there was little point hiding anything from her dad. While her mother was the driven one who made sure the hotel turned in the profits, he had always been the people person who smoothed connections and made relationships. Now he had grown frail, and had to pace himself carefully, and Sadie wondered what exactly caused her mother to keep working quite so hard after her husband of thirty years had nearly died. But even though he had grown physically frail, his mind remained as sharp and perceptive as ever.

"Just thinking through a few things, and decisions to be made."

"Come and see us when you can. I will try to make sure your mother's free."

Sadie laughed. It was a family joke, even though she wasn't sure her mother appreciated it. Then they chatted for a few more minutes and afterwards Sadie decided the flat wasn't quite as lonely or silent as she had feared.

The next morning, while Sadie was tackling the backlog of emails, Adam made sure he was in work early. Even so, he was the last one of the team to arrive. DI Will Spencer had been working through the night, and the greying blond stubble revealed he hadn't had a chance to shave for quite a few days. DS Emma Sutton and DC Wayne Whittington were hunkered down in front of a screen in one corner, while in the other DC Stuart Sawyer and DC Maria Watson were just settling down to work on a cold case which had suddenly become surprisingly warm.

"Glad you could join us," said DI Spencer, downing the remains of a very strong dark coffee, "morning briefing starts in five minutes."

"Good morning to you," said Adam. "Can I grab you for a moment?"

"It better not be one of your bloody hunches," said DI Spencer, the effort of the past twenty-four hours showing through, "I'm going home after the morning briefing to grab a couple of hours' kip."

"No, but you better be sitting down when I tell you what it is."

"Two minutes, then," said DI Spencer ushering him into his office where the odour of last night's curry hung heavy in the already foetid atmosphere.

"So, then," he said, easing himself into the chair, "what's the big news?"

"How about a body under the patio?"

"You're kidding, right?"

"No, talk to DI Gregory at Peninsula if you don't believe me. I thought you should know before the news leaks out."

DI Spencer burst out laughing. "That is f***ing brilliant. We are slammed up to our eyeballs, and my officer returns with a body under the patio. That has so made my day."

Put that way, Adam found it hard not to share his inspector's black sense of humour. "Of course, from a professional point of view it's none of my business."

"Absolutely," said Will, suddenly regaining his composure, "and you can't afford to get distracted. While you've been away dealing with bodies, we've been looking again at the intel. We still don't have the proof, but what's going on at Stan Collins' place smells even worse than this office."

"That's saying something," said Adam, more loudly than he intended.

"It's good to have you back. Right, onto the morning briefing."

As the weary team finished sharing the fruit of their labours, DS Hezekiah from the Drugs Squad joined them. He was a stocky, heavily tattooed individual in his mid 30s, with heavy eyebrows and short, curly, dark hair, and his brief was to share the details of the stakeout at the fish shop (not that this establishment sold steak, he said, punning feebly). There was a maisonette at the rear of the chip shop. The ground floor was occupied by one of the original inhabitants of the estate, who very much kept herself to herself, and was rather hard of hearing. Upstairs there were two floors that had been vacant for nearly a year; there had been a water leak the housing association had been dilatory in fixing, and both were in need of redecorating. The equipment was set up and ready to go, and after much wrangling money had been found to fund a month's surveillance.

Adam raised the issue of the housing manager.

DS Hezekiah smiled. "He's no longer a problem. Moved in with his sister in Norwich, I believe. No, we have arranged it all with Chloe. Her brother's a police officer so she should be secure."

Adam thought of Carl Carter and his sidekick Frank Fogarty, and once again he reflected how much his job eroded confidence in human nature. But there was no reason, as far as he was aware, to distrust DS Tunde Hezekiah, and trying to keep an open mind, he headed out to the property, knowing that soon he would become a very close colleague indeed.

Chapter 11

THE FIRST FEW DAYS AT the maisonette passed painfully slowly. The Great Jones Fish Fryer had as a culinary establishment hardly enough custom to be financially viable. It opened for a couple of hours at lunchtime to feed a few regulars. It then remained closed until 5pm when young families would come for their tea. Afterwards, as evening wore on, the grey tracksuits gathered. Some came on foot, some on bicycle, a few older ones had mopeds. They generally hung around the back of the shop to vape or smoke, or to hang with the girls, and from time to time a couple would go off on their own, to the amusement of everyone else.

Then the day's trading was done, and after all the chores were completed, Stan Collins would retreat to his second floor flat, where he seemed to lead a quiet, uneventful life. And what happened on the floor below was equally uninteresting. It was officially Grease's residence but each night he left on his motorbike, to an as yet unknown location, leaving Tunde and Adam staring at a black, empty space.

During these long slow hours, Tunde and Adam tried their hardest to build a friendship. But they had little in common. Tunde was an adrenaline junkie, with a passion for Mixed Martial Arts. Adam spent his day job investigating assaults and he didn't want to spend his free time being reminded of them. Tunde had numerous girlfriends around

London, and he couldn't understand why Adam wasn't playing the field when his girlfriend was so far away. There was the football and the news, of course, but even so they often found they were making conversation for the sake of conversation.

So there was plenty of time to think. Adam still hadn't found the answer to the tangled web of relationships on the estate. What linked Carl Carter with Stan Collins? Where was Grease's mother? And who was Lewis Sinclair anyway? Tunde couldn't help, and Adam was anxious to have some time back in the office to find out more. But that piece of the investigation would just have to wait.

Then there was his own family. He knew he could never fully know, but he couldn't help wondering what DI Gregory and the team were unearthing at Netherworthy Lodge. That solicitor's letter had plunged him into another world where one strange discovery had followed another, and at the heart of it was a relative called David Pennycome he now realised he hardly knew.

So much was going through Adam's head. He found some relief in the Bible app Sadie had helped him install on his phone. There was a verse of Scripture each day and even though Adam didn't always understand it, the words gave him a measure of peace and comfort – that is, until he started thinking of Sadie.

As for Sadie, a weekend off had led to a backlog in orders, and she scarcely had a free moment as she immersed herself in her burgeoning business. Her evening with Damien was almost an inconvenience, but it was a commitment she could not avoid. So on the Thursday evening she pulled up as promised outside his flat. Damien was already waiting, his usual cheery, charming self. He gave her a peck on the cheek and then started to talk about his favourite subject, yours truly. Sadie, however, knew him well enough to realise that underneath the facade Damien was nervous.

Still, the environment at the church suited him. It was a large, comfortably furnished venue that reminded Sadie more of the Korean church she had attended in Australia than any place of worship she had so far encountered back home. It was full of keen, young professionals all rather like Damien except they talked more about Jesus than themselves. And the catering was of an exceptional standard. A team of willing interns served a three course dinner from a fully kitted kitchen that the rest of the week, apparently, was used to feed the homeless.

But the evening was more than just the food. Over coffee a video was shown. It was of a rich man in a hot air balloon, and the theme was whether it was possible to serve God and money. A time of discussion then followed, and everyone was encouraged to participate. Damien, however, was clearly reluctant to say anything, although he listened politely enough. As for Sadie, her mind was elsewhere. She was the person in the hot air balloon, she was the one believing in her own serene progress, as she floated on the currents of her own dreams and ambitions. But now she saw that at some point or other, her balloon had to land, and it was time to decide where.

For very different reasons, therefore, Damien and Sadie made their excuses and left early. They arrived back at Damien's flat, not having said very much.

"Don't you want to come in for a coffee?" asked Damien, touching her knee.

"I don't think so," said Sadie.

"No offence taken, I hope," said Damien.

Sadie smiled as she drove away. Damien had turned up at school in the sixth form. He had lived in various countries across the world, and he was a smooth, confident storyteller with a charm few could resist. He studied the same subjects as Sadie, and when they ended up at the same university they had for a couple of heady months lived together. But when the charm wore off, Sadie quickly realised sex with Damien was all about his needs, his desires and she had politely ended the relationship. From that time on, she had saved herself, waiting for the right man. That is, until it came to that night with Adam…

Sadie realised she had almost passed her parking space and as she reversed cautiously, she suddenly remembered, with a pang of regret, she hadn't yet phoned Jo. Fortunately, Jo seemed very understanding and they soon made plans to meet up the following weekend in Oxford. "It will be a real pleasure," said Jo, and Sadie wondered just how much pleasure Jo ever experienced. They continued chatting for a while but eventually the call had to end. And as Sadie turned her attention back to more emails she could only wonder what Adam was doing that night.

At that precise moment Stan was emptying the rubbish into a large bin in the back alley. Then as every other night he locked up and made his way upstairs. But something that night was different. The light in Grease's flat was on, and he hadn't left on his motorbike. Tunde and Adam watched, waited, anticipated. But the minutes went by, then an hour, then another.

Just as Tunde and Adam's attention was beginning to wane, a small van appeared beneath them. A quick ANPR check revealed it had been hired in the Felixstowe area. At the same, some grey tracksuits appeared from the shadows, and began to unload what looked like boxes of packaging material. They went inside, and through the curtains Tunde and Adam could see movement in Grease's flat. The van disappeared, and for the next hour or so calm descended on the alley.

Then the army of cyclists appeared. In what was clearly a well drilled operation, they went upstairs and returned a few minutes later to disappear back into the darkness. Each had a rucksack of some kind, so it was impossible to tell what was in any of them, or whether anything had been added. But even so, Adam knew they contained more than soup and sandwiches.

His mind wandered back to Niall O'connor, and he wondered how many more vulnerable individuals were about to receive an unwelcome visitor. "Too many," said Tunde, "and one's too many."

The detectives sent their footage off to the digital lab. They watched and waited to see if anything else happened. But all was quiet, that night and the night after. They suspected the drugs' drop happened weekly, "Just in time for the weekend," as Tunde put it. But both knew they had to stay vigilant, just in case any fresh details emerged.

So night after night rolled by until the following Tuesday. Tunde and Adam were as usual trying to stimulate each other with some conversation, and Tunde was leading a discussion on American football when a call came in from Blessing McQueen. There had been an attempted mugging in the underpass near Magnolia House. Only, the intended victim was a martial arts instructor. One lad had cycled away furiously but she had disarmed and detained the other one, while a passer-by phoned the police. She had suffered a wound to the shoulder, but nothing a few stitches could not mend.

"I would very much like to attend the interview tomorrow," said Adam.

"Thought you would," said Blessing in that light, clear voice he found almost irresistible. "We'll hold him overnight while we sort out the paperwork, and I will see you about ten."

"Perfect," said Adam. If Blessing ever wanted a promotion, he decided he would be the first to recommend her.

"I've got this," said Tunde, "if you need to grab some kip."

Adam needed no second invitation. Even though he could work all night, he could feel his body relaxing at the thought of a sensible bedtime.

The next day the cares of the world seemed to weigh less heavy as Adam made his way to work. The days were drawing in, and first light was just breaking over all the familiar landmarks, grey at first, then slowly turning a rusty orange, before finally settling into a crisp, clear blue that spoke of cooler weather to come. Adam by this time had almost arrived. He took a lungful of air before entering, and thought for a moment about the sunrise in Little Netherworthy.

But today he needed to be focused. PC McQueen did a thoroughly professional job of briefing him, and together they agreed an interview strategy. It was still only half past nine, however, and the duty solicitor was running late. So Adam took the opportunity to do some further research into Carol Sinclair. His research into family history had taught him to look further back along the generations. And there she was, Carol's mother, Joan Lewis, still alive and living appropriately enough in Lewisham. So that explained Grease's name. But could it also explain something else?

On a whim, Adam started searching for women called Carol Lewis. And there, after some digging, was the daughter, living and working on a caravan park in Cornwall. So what had caused her to abandon everything and start all over? Was she really free of her old life or was she still in touch with her son? He was desperate to find out more, but as DI Spencer agreed, he could hardly ask her without compromising the whole investigation.

"Sir," said Blessing, "the interview's ready."

The lad in question was thirteen. He was thin, with blotchy, pale skin, and he had a cold. His mother said nothing as he regularly wiped his nose with the back of his hand, and indeed she seemed completely disinterested in the whole proceedings.

Blessing laid out piece by piece the facts of what happened. To each question the boy nervously mumbled, "No comment," glancing from time to time not at his mother but the duty solicitor, who looked back at him less than sympathetically.

Blessing having finished, it was Adam's turn.

"So who told you to steal the phones?"

"No comment," said the boy, tugging at a piece of loose skin on his knuckle.

"What will happen to you now that you've failed in your mission?"

A look of alarm spread over the boy's face. "N-n-n-no comment," he stammered. But to Adam it sounded more like a cry for help.

Adam shrugged his shoulders. "If you don't tell us, there's nothing we can do."

He abruptly terminated the interview. The lad, called Kevin, opened his mouth but no sound came out. He was paler than ever now and visibly shaking.

"Sometimes," said Adam afterwards, "no comments tell you all you need to know."

"Agreed," said Blessing. "Should I phone social services?"

"Good idea, and if you can, keep an eye on him. I think he's about to have a very rough time of it."

As Adam made his way back to the maisonette, he found himself thinking about his thirteen year old self. He had done some stupid things back then to impress his mates without, however, breaking the law. But then his old man had sat him down and told him, "Son, you're a Pennycome. Pennycomes don't need to prove themselves to no-one." And that was the one piece of advice that Adam had always heeded from that point on. Somehow someone needed to have a similar chat with Kevin, and soon. If indeed, it wasn't too late.

Chapter 12

ON THE FRIDAY OF THAT week the first named storm of the year broke over the British Isles. It started with a brisk wind and a few heavy raindrops, just as the cyclists turned up at the maisonette to take delivery of their packages. By the morning, down in the Southwest, there was torrential rain and flooding.

DI Gregory sighed. He had planned to take the train, but as always happened in such weather, the railway line was out of action. So he would have to drive, and avoid the idiots who usually caused crashes in such conditions. As he joined the motorway, a car whizzed down the fast line far in excess of the speed limit, even though the warning signs were flashing at 50.

As he made his way determinedly towards the capital, DI Gregory thought of his recent encounter with DS Pennycome. Even though he had not yet formally interviewed him, he sensed Adam was a man who could be relied upon to do a thoroughly professional job. There was a vacancy coming up in the department next year – would young Adam want to move down here and apply for the post? The answer, he supposed, would very much depend on what he told him today.

The storm was just starting to ease as DI Gregory made his wearisome way through the London traffic to the police station. He related instantly to the same tired facade, the same tatty decor, and the same forlorn notices in the foyer that only interested the bored and the insane. At least down in his part of the world there was, at least on the top floor, the view of rolling green hills and a distant promise of freedom. Here, as far as he could tell, there was no view other than the adjacent industrial estate or a row of equally depressing office blocks, also in desperate need of repair.

Still, the stairwell had recently had a lick of paint, and on the landing stood a rather garish aquarium where a selection of brightly coloured fish enjoyed their watery prison. But DI Gregory was not here to admire the decor. He was led through the wooden doors, through a rather untidy office into a cramped, dark room, where his counterpart DI Will Spencer was sitting. They chatted briefly for a few minutes, about the forthcoming pay review, about a couple of policy changes that needed implementing, about the weather, and then DS Adam Pennycome joined them.

"Sorry, I'm late," said Adam, squeezing carefully onto the third chair that just about fitted behind the door. "I've just got back from our surveillance op."

"How's it going?" asked DI Gregory sympathetically, rather glad such operations were now generally behind him.

"You know – generally long and boring. But we are collecting some useful evidence."

"I need to have a word with you about the results from the digital lab," said DI Spencer, "but that can wait until later."

Adam nodded, and it was clear to DI Gregory that despite the conditions, there was a good working atmosphere in this team. He added that detail to his mental portrait of DS Pennycome and stored it away, just in case that application ever came in. For now, there was work to be done, and the sooner it was over, the sooner he could get home. He had never liked staying in London, and today definitely was no exception.

"So let me tell you about your unwelcome guest," explained DI Gregory, "we have an ID. We noticed the unusual dental pattern early on, which helped. It led us to confirm that our body is Timmy Taylor who was last seen leaving a pub in Exeter in June 1990. The question then is, who put Timmy Taylor under your patio?"

"Are you able to tell me?" asked Adam, taking a long slurp of coffee.

"Well, I reckon you'll find out soon enough, and I think I can trust you enough not to go rogue. From the paperwork in the garage it seems the lodge was let out at that time to someone called Billy Hurst until October. We haven't been able to establish anything positive about Mr Hurst, and we haven't been able so far to get much out of forensics. But as your great-uncle was living in Hungary until just before Christmas that year, our Billy must remain the chief suspect."

Adam knew that legally his great-uncle's innocence hadn't been proven beyond doubt. But even so a wave of relief came unbidden over him, and he found himself smiling at his boss. He, however, remained impassive and stayed focused on what his counterpart was saying.

"Of course I haven't come all this way to tell you that. The reason why I am here, however, is that Timmy Taylor's parents still live in the capital, and out of courtesy I wondered if DS Pennycome would be able to come with me."

Will nodded and after Adam and Charlie had established first-name terms, they crawled through fume-filled streets in a dreary drizzle until they reached a corner of London Adam barely knew existed. Charlie turned into a street of newish brick boxes, where heavy brown paint was already peeling from the windows, and satellite dishes were streaked with rust and grime. Mr and Mrs Taylor lived in number 32, only distinguishable by the faded welcome mat outside for the son who would never come home.

Adam always hated this part of the job: the awkward small talk while the obligatory cup of tea was brewed; the parents positioning themselves awkwardly on the sofa, hand in hand; the shock and the tears, sometimes silent, sometimes loud and violent, as the news was broken. Eric and Dawn Taylor were no exceptions. At least they were still together, thought Adam, even though the stress of the past three decades was etched deeply into their expressions.

"So how did you find him?" asked Eric quietly.

Charlie looked at Adam.

"An accidental discovery at a family property," Adam improvised unconvincingly.

"That means you know the bastard who did this."

"Sadly no," replied Charlie, "but we are following a number of leads. Did Timmy tell you about friends he met before he died?"

Eric shook his head. "Timmy never told us very much," said Dawn, "he always was a free spirit. Me and Eric, we were brought up proper, strict, like. We wanted something different for Timmy, let him choose the path he wanted."

"Fine good that did us," muttered Eric, but his wife ignored him and carried on. "Sometimes he brought home girlfriends, sometimes he brought home boyfriends."

"And what took him to Exeter?" asked Charlie.

"He was running away," said Eric. "Bloody fool, if you ask me. Found someone who really cared for him, and he took off as fast as he could."

Adam nearly said something, but checked himself long enough for Charlie to carry on. "So when did you last speak to Timmy?"

"The previous Christmas," said Eric sadly. "We'd had a row about money. Timmy was expecting a hand-out as usual, and well, I'd just lost my job and we didn't have any to spare."

"We did tell Timmy how much we loved him and told him we would help, if we could."

"Aye," said Eric turning to his wife, "but that wasn't good enough for Timmy. We heard bugger all from him until this policeman knocks on our door at the start of July and tells us he is missing."

Dawn began to weep silently again, and Eric mechanically took her hand.

"Just a couple more questions," said Charlie downing his steeped, acidic tea. "Timmy was working in a pub at the time of his disappearance. Do you know anything at all about what he was doing?"

"No," said Eric quietly. "Like I said to you, Timmy told us nothing."

"Does the name Billy Hurst mean anything to you?"

"Is he a suspect?" asked Eric.

"Not necessarily," replied Charlie. "If, however, you remember anything or want any further support, DS Pennycome will be pleased to assist."

Adam pulled out his card and gave it to Dawn who smiled weakly. "When can we have the funeral?" she whispered.

"Not for a while yet," said Charlie, "but as soon as we can, we will let you know."

At this point, the two detectives stood up and said their farewells. Eric saw them to the door and gently closed it behind them.

Adam realised there was little point in Charlie driving back to the station. The journey back to Devon would be long enough that evening without any diversions. He thanked Charlie for the invitation to the interview and was about to head off to the nearest tube station, when Charlie suddenly said, "I nearly forgot. I have something in the boot. Nothing to do with the enquiry but I think it will interest you."

He produced an old, faded carrier bag. "Found it at the bottom of one of the boxes destined for the tip. I am not sure whether your great-uncle meant to throw it away."

"I'll have a look," said Adam, intrigued.

Later that evening Adam carefully went through the contents. There were letters, dated from 1977-78, in a woman's handwriting. Adam guessed they were in German. There was a newspaper cutting, and wrapped very delicately in a wad of tissue paper a pressed blue flower. "You sly old dog," said Adam. "Now perhaps we will find out who you really are."

There was just time before he headed out again to ring his sister. Jo, for her part, was already on her way to bed, determined to be awake and alert enough to enjoy her unexpected day out in Oxford, and she had just poured herself a stiff nightcap as Adam called. But she really did not mind the interruption. This kind of mystery appealed to her imagination, and it was the sort of material that maybe, just maybe, the aspiring writer deep inside her would one day be able to use. So it was agreed: Adam would drop off the letters on the way back from the maisonette in the morning, and Jo would translate them just as soon as she could. Quite what the result of her efforts would be, that was something, however, neither of them could at that stage predict.

Chapter 13

AFTER MUCH NEGOTIATION WITH DI Spencer and DS Sutton, Adam had finally secured a weekend off. There had been a slight dip in the caseload, and now seemed as good a time as any to argue for the ever willing Wayne Whittington to gain some experience of surveillance work – besides, his overtime rate was considerably lower.

Adam knew he was tired, as the times of his recent runs testified. Yet as always happened in the middle of an investigation, his mind would still be working hard, mulling over the questions constantly running in the background. Where exactly did Grease go each night? What was the relationship like with his mother? And how exactly did he fund his lifestyle? Hopefully in the coming week there would be some answers, and about time too. The operation couldn't go on much longer, but the team needed to be fully prepared before they could make their move.

But this time there were also the personal questions adding to the fatigue. Was there enough evidence to bring a case against Billy Hurst? And if not, what would the CPS decide? And beyond all that, there was the figure of Uncle David whom Adam was learning was a considerably more complex character than he had previously realised. Surely an ex-copper would at least have had some suspicions about a tenant building a patio in such an unusual place?

He was still thinking about his great-uncle as he delivered his letters to his sister. She lived in a room on the first floor of a dilapidated Victorian property, partly hidden behind a barricade of green and brown Wheelie bins. Someone had left evidence of last night's party on the pavement outside, and even at this early hour her infamous noisy neighbours were clearly generating their own rhythm to a heavy techno bass.

Jo clearly deserved better than this. She was still in her dressing gown, deciding what to wear for the grand day out. "Have fun," said Adam. "I will," said Jo, who had fought off her headache with strong painkillers. She took the bag eagerly and promised to look at it on the journey. Then she paused for a moment and asked hesitantly, "Do you think Uncle David wanted us to know about the letters?"

"He could've destroyed them years ago," replied Adam, who had thought exactly the same thing. "As it is, however, I am sure we would have found the evidence sooner or later."

"This isn't another one of your cases," laughed Jo, and Adam realised how long it was since he had seen her smile.

"I suppose not," he said with a rueful grin, "at least, I hope not."

"Go on with you. I have a train to catch."

"Love you, sis," said Adam, giving her a hug on the way out. "And," he added, "give Sadie my love…"

At that very moment Sadie was already on the train towards Oxford, working, as always, on her trusty laptop, answering emails, processing orders, updating her accounts. She had long realised her growing business generated enough work for two, yet only paid enough to support one member of staff. The question she could not answer was how she could continue expanding operations if she and Adam ever got together… if indeed that ever happened. She typed away mechanically while her thoughts were far away, drawing up and rejecting a multitude of scenarios that presented themselves, finding herself as far away from a solution as ever.

Eventually, however, as the train drew into Oxford, Sadie packed her laptop away, and focused on the day ahead with his sister Jo. Truth be told, she really wasn't sure how the time would go with this curious, shy creature she didn't really know that well. She expected a waif trailing behind the crowds, anxious about seeing her. But to her surprise Jo was positively marching out at the front of the throng. Her hair had recently been expertly styled. She was wearing a long blue cardigan and flowing denim skirt, with a grey scarf tucked round her neck that matched her eyes, and ankle length tan boots. When she saw Sadie she waved and almost began to run.

"Hello," said Jo, clearly excited.

"Hello," said Sadie. "You look amazing."

"Let's grab a coffee. I have something amazing to share."

A quarter of an hour later they were seated in a quiet corner of the cafe at Oxford Castle, beneath the picture of a scruffy Victorian urchin sentenced to hard labour for her crimes. On the way Jo told Sadie about the carrier bag and how she had begun translating the letters on the way, and how she had nearly missed her stop. Sadie never realised Jo could talk, and guessed it was a rare opportunity for her to do so. She didn't mind really, and it meant that she wouldn't have to manufacture conversation today.

So, as Sadie took Jo's order and queued for their coffees, she formulated a plan. Jo would translate each letter and she would take down her dictation. That way they could send whatever information they discovered direct to Adam, if indeed it was important. Little did she realise that three hours and one lunch later she would only just be finished.

"Can I just double check what you have written?" asked Jo.

"Be my guest. I'm going to toast Uncle David with another cup of coffee."

Dear David,

I don't know if this letter will reach you or if you even remember me. My mind tells me I am foolish even daring to write, but my heart says I must, and you know my heart of old.

My husband Erwald has come home today from a trade fair in Vienna. He said he met a salesman from England who spoke in a Styrian accent. I asked how that was possible, as most Englishmen do not even speak High German. Then he said that this gentleman had served with the Military Police here in Graz over twenty years ago. I hope he did not see the look of surprise on my face at this point. I asked what he was doing at a trade fair and Erwald said that he had recently left the police and was selling copying machines. He also said he had a funny name. I knew then what he was about to say, and I made as if to cough so I could go to the bathroom and get a glass of water.

When my husband was asleep, I went downstairs into my husband's office and found your name on a list of delegates staying at the Kaiserhof Hotel. Please forgive my foolishness, but I would like so much to see you one more time. I am going to see my cousin in Vienna next Saturday. There is a coffee house just outside the station by the name of Becker. I will be there at eleven o'clock and I will wait one hour for you.

I do not know if fate has brought us together again. Next Saturday I will find out.

My thoughts still remain with you,
Claudia Bach (formerly Nagy)

Dearest David,

I waited and I waited, and I thought you would never come. But at half eleven there you were! I cannot believe it is twenty-two years since we last saw each other. And yet I recognised you at once. You still walk like a soldier, and you still have that warm smile that captured my heart all that time ago.

I was sad that we had so little time to talk. You told me all about England, and how it is not the same country you served with honour back in the 50s. You talked about the power cuts, and the strikes, and the punk rockers. You said how you gave up being a policeman when you were hurt on the picket line, and that is when you decided to start travelling for a living. But life today cannot be so bad can it?

Certainly, I would very much like you to come and see Graz as it is now. We have rebuilt our city, and we no longer go to bed hungry at night. We are still afraid of the Russians, but they are no longer threatening to march into our city at any moment. My husband and I have a pretty little house in the neighbourhood of Eggenberg and a garden full of roses that is my pride and joy.

Since we met, so many memories of our time together have come back to me. Last night I dreamt that once again we were walking by the River Mur in the pouring rain, and you were laughing at the words of the folksong I was teaching you. You made me so happy then, and I would love to have the opportunity to share our memories one more time.

If you want to write to me, I have a godmother nearby who is almost blind. Sometimes I have letters and parcels sent there when I want to give Erwald a surprise. Please do send me a letter soon to let me know if you can come.

I look forward very much to hearing from you,
Claudia.

Dearest David,

I know that you travel much on business, so you must not apologise that it has taken so long for you to write. I am only glad that you have written to me.

You ask about my husband. He is an honest and true man who has always taken good care of me. But he does not understand matters of the heart. I have not spoken to him about you, and it is best that you do not meet him.

He is going away for a sales conference in Hamburg in a month's time. Please do come for the weekend if you can. There is a guesthouse not too far from here where you can stay.

There are so many things I want to say, but I find I cannot write them down in a letter.

Your loving friend,

Claudia

My darling David,

I am so looking forward to you coming next week. I will be waiting outside the station. I cannot believe that after all these years you are finally coming back to Graz.

Do you remember the night we spent in the woods near Weiz? I was shy and nervous at first, but you were so gentle with me, as always. I will never forget your soft kisses and your strong embrace. When we woke up just before dawn, I asked why I couldn't marry you. You said you would soon be moving on, and I had to stay behind and look after my mother. You were right of course – my mother and I were the only ones who survived the war, but I still cried. Then you dried my tears, and told me you wanted to see the sunrise with me one last time. So we put on our clothes and walked hand in hand through damp, dewy meadows to the top of a nearby hill. I was cold – my dress was so shabby and thin – but you held me so tight, and I wished the moment could last forever. It was just you and me, listening to the birds greeting the rising sun. There was a cuckoo, I remember, and a pair of thrushes, and you said you could hear a robin. I knew that you were saying goodbye, but I always hoped that when we said "Auf wiederschauen" we really would see each other again.

I am literally counting down the hours.

With much anticipation,

Claudia

David, my heart,

What a wonderful, magical weekend we spent together! I almost felt like I was eighteen years old again and in love for the very first time again, especially when you told me you still had the gentian I picked on our very last morning. Only I am sure that back then the steps up the Schlossberg were not as steep, and I did not have to stop for breath at the top.

The sight from the top is impressive, isn't it? The brick red roof tops and the narrow streets looked so pretty in the summer sunshine, and beyond the old city Graz is stretching out so far. I can see why you found it hard to recognise it from the bombed out ruins you remember. There are no longer barefoot children roaming the streets or refugees too frightened to speak of the horrors they have seen. So much good has happened in the last quarter of a century, and I am glad that your visit has put some of your memories to rest.

When I next go to Vienna, I will get the photos of our time together developed and send them to you: the site of the school where you were stationed, now turned into flats; our walk in the grounds of Eggenberg castle; you and I eating ice cream beneath the clock tower of the

Schlossberg. For my part, I hardly need the photos. These pictures are already stored in my memories, and I will treasure them always.

In the meanwhile, I do not want Erwald to find out what has happened between us. He suspects nothing, and I learnt long ago how to play the role of the dutiful wife. In my own kind of way, I suppose I love him, but not in the same way I love you still.

You have said this is the last time you will visit Graz and although my heart is heavy, I think your decision is right. I sometimes ask myself how life would have turned out if our fate had been different. But you cannot waste your time away wondering. I have been asked to sing my folksongs next week at a charity event and I am already practising! No-one there will guess, however, who I will be thinking of when I am singing.

Yours forever,

Claudia

Dearest David,

I do not know how to say this. I have the most unexpected news – I am pregnant! Many years ago the doctor told me I could never have a child and now I am forty I thought my dream of becoming a mother was over. I cannot in all honesty tell who the father is. Whatever the truth, I know that Erwald will be delighted to have a child to call his own, and I am delighted that I can give Erwald this opportunity. I could never leave him, and he is exactly the sort of man you said I should marry.

I have decided, however, that if my child should turn out to look like you, I will tell Erwald that he takes after my father who disappeared during the war. All our family photos were destroyed when our home in Szombathely was bombed, and I have nothing to remind me of his appearance, except some faint memories from when I was eight years old. So I may not be telling a complete lie.

I think the time has come now for me to stop writing. I have destroyed all your letters so there is never a chance they can be discovered. Know that wherever you go, part of me goes with you. Never stop being gentle and kind, and I pray that God grants you the happiness you deserve.

Yours forever,

Claudia

1st February 1978 To Erwald Heinrich and Claudia Radegund Bach, a son Thomas David, a wonderful blessing and a much wished-for child.

Sadie handed Jo the last cup of coffee. "Happy?" she said.

"Yes," said Jo, "I think that's a fair translation. I wonder what Adam will make of our uncle's little secret."

"Well, let's press send and find out," said Sadie smiling. Then she added rather seriously, "You know, it all seems fairly abusive to me."

"What do you mean?"

"Soldier marches into town, sees a pretty girl, takes advantage of her. It's the same story the world over. Then he leaves, and all that's left is a broken heart and a sadder, wiser woman."

"Yet it was Claudia who sought him out all those years later."

"Some people," said Sadie firmly, "have trouble separating reality from fantasy. In a marriage like hers the fantasy David really loved her was what kept her going. The reality was, they had a brief fling and who's to know if this was either first or last time he carved a notch on his bedpost. Sadly, Claudia just couldn't see that. To her he was, and always would be, her knight in shining armour."

"Shall I settle up?" asked Jo. She detected a vehement undercurrent in Sadie's words, probably from her own bitter experience, and she wasn't sure how to carry on the conversation.

"I've got this," said Sadie more softly, in a reconciliatory tone.

The two of them wandered slowly through the city centre, window shopping, then past the colleges down to the Botanic Gardens. As they were drinking iced tea down by the river, Sadie suddenly asked Jo, "Have you ever been stalked?"

"Not me – I've spent most of my life being invisible. But I had friends at uni who were, and it was the most horrible experience. Is that what happened to you?"

Sadie fixed Jo with her clear emerald eyes. "Yes – for a whole year. I don't really want to go into details, but someone called Tucker Magee made my life a misery. Fortunately, he's history now, but even now I carry the scars."

"What do you mean?"

"Your brother is the most amazing and the most loyal person I've ever known," said Sadie, getting straight to the point. "But it's taking a long time to learn to trust again, and I'm only very slowly getting there."

"How much does Adam know?"

"Not much. I know, I know, I need to tell him soon, and I will. But I hope you can see why I wanted to speak with you first. I'm not being unreasonable, am I?"

Jo shook her head. She was only grateful Sadie had chosen to confide in her, and she was only too glad to listen. "Just let him know the wait will be worth it," she said quietly and gently squeezed her hand.

"I will," promised Sadie who in turn gave her a kiss. Then they sat for a little while longer in the unseasonably warm autumn sunshine, watching the world go by, and chatting about the places they had visited, until Sadie suddenly realised she had to get back for her brother Kevin's birthday.

"Let me know what you find out about your family," she said as they said their goodbyes.

"I will definitely keep in touch," replied Jo, and then, thinking of her noisy neighbours, headed off to the nearest bookshop to stay as long as possible, or at least until closing time.

Chapter 14

"I ALWAYS KNEW MY UNCLE was a dark horse. Everyone else was fooled by his bachelor ways, but not me. I saw what I saw."

"And what did you see, Dad?"

"An old man with an eye for the ladies, if you know what I mean."

"Did you know he had a child?"

"As I say, he was a dark horse. Never thought he'd shack up with a German, though."

"She was Austrian."

"German, Austrian, same difference. So you're going to track this bird down?"

"She's in her early eighties now, and no, Germany and Austria are very different."

"Yeah, well, I know my history. But I guess they taught you different at university, always filling your head with nonsense."

"Perhaps you can share your version of history when you get to meet her."

"And why would I want to do that? No, the person Mum and I are really interested in is this girlfriend you keep talking about. After all this time, don't you think we should've met her by now?"

Adam was still thinking about this conversation with his father when he woke up the following morning. According to Jo, the day with Sadie went well, but that was all she was prepared to say. Sadie herself had been in touch, and Adam had promised a meet up as soon as there was a break in the investigation. So the signs were encouraging, although there was no way he was going to inflict his parents on her anytime soon.

He went down to the gym and worked out for a good hour. It was good simply to concentrate on the needs of his body, and drown out the many questions he could not answer. Then on a whim he went off and found a church.

The service was of a completely different scale to that down in Little Netherworthy. There was a congregation of several hundred, who seemed to move in one choreographed motion. The music was led by a band of professionally trained musicians, broadcast around the building and online on the very latest technology.

Adam felt like the proverbial fish out of water, and yet even though he understood very little, he recognised something good was going on. There was a concise, clear sermon at the end to round off the worship, on the subject of something called a covenant, where the preacher taught about the nature and the cost of unconditional commitment. He was talking about God, of course, but at that moment Adam couldn't help thinking about his relationship with Sadie.

He would have lingered longer afterwards, and maybe grabbed a coffee, but Jo was already waiting at his flat. She made no response to Adam's excuse when he turned up, keys in hand, and in that moment Adam reflected how hard it was for his generation to grasp the concept of going to church. Church had no connection at all with the world they lived in, it was an irrelevance, a relic of a bygone age, and Jo's blank look was in many ways the expected response.

Jo for her part was merely looking forward to having lunch with her brother, something which recently had been a rare treat indeed, and tracking down the mysterious Claudia Radegund Bach. So over meatballs and spaghetti, they started the search. She was forty in 1977, so she had to be in her early eighties now, if indeed she was still alive. And what about her husband Erwald? Patiently Adam and Jo searched the death announcements in the local media, and there was Erwald Bach, retired sales manager, late of Eggenberg, survived by his loving wife Claudia, and devoted son, Thomas. So where was Claudia? Further digging eventually yielded an address in that district, and although there were plenty of other women with that name, this was the only one they could find there. But was there any other evidence? Yes, remarkably it seemed this Claudia was still teaching singing and she described herself as a former music teacher.

"So what do we do now?" asked Jo.

Adam thought for a moment. "How about an all-expenses paid trip to Graz?"

"And what? Just knock on her door?"

"Why not? I find the direct approach always works the best."

Jo sighed. Bravery was not her strong point, but she recognised the truth of Adam's words. "I'll sort it out at work tomorrow." Then she added, "Truth be told, I probably need to have a break. My managers are talking about making me redundant and offering a freelance contract. I'm not sure where that leaves me, or whether I can still afford to live in London."

"That's tough," said Adam, sympathetically. He and Jo both knew Dad and Mum were helping their sister Sally, whom they were seeing later. But Sally had always been their parents' favourite, and they pretty much expected Jo to make her own way in the world. So as so often, it would be up to him to provide any assistance she needed. The unfairness of it all still angered him, but he knew there was little he could say to them that could improve the situation.

"Don't worry, I'll be fine," said Jo, who hated being dependent on anybody. "So, shall we look up flights to Graz?"

As they began to make plans, Adam realised that the cares and worries of the ongoing investigation were beginning to recede into the background. Yet he also was acutely aware such a respite was but a moment of calm before the inevitable storm, and he remembered the chaos he walked into the previous Monday morning. So the next day, he took care to get up even earlier than usual, to make sure this time he was seen to be punctual and prompt.

As it turned out, Adam was the first in, and the office seemed almost quiet. DC Wayne Whittington was eager to debrief him, of course, but the weekend surveillance had really only confirmed what Adam already knew. So before heading out on the lunchtime shift, Adam began to concentrate his efforts on gathering intelligence on Grease. Uniform had tracked him down to an address in North London. It seemed to be an ordinary two-bedroom flat in a fairly ordinary neighbourhood, and there were no markers on the property that indicated the presence of weapons or drugs.

But Adam knew well enough by now it was this very appearance of ordinariness that demanded the most attention. So who owned the flat? Apparently some investment company. Well, that was nothing unusual, especially in London. But where was this company based? This was where it became interesting. Even though the late Niall O'connor may not have realised it, his flat in Magnolia House was the registered address. So, it had to be presumed, anyone involved in this company would somehow have to be connected with the Great Jones Street drugs ring. OK, then who was the director?

This is where Adam hit a blank for now. If the paperwork was to be believed, the man behind it all was a certain Shane Stephens. But Adam was pretty sure his official particulars were fake – unless he really did live in an industrial estate in Stratford. Perhaps there was a clue in his date of birth, sometime in 1965, but that did not match the age of Carl Carter (dec'd) or Stan Collins or anyone else so far unearthed during the operation.

Adam looked up at the clock. He needed to get back to his watching brief with DS Tunde Hezekiah. But first he needed to make a couple of phone calls. First of all, he left a message with Chloe at the housing association to see if any company paperwork had turned up at Magnolia House. Then, he phoned the bank again for the financial information he had demanded a fortnight ago for Lewis Sinclair. By now, his sense of frustration was growing, and when the young call handler claimed ignorance of the whole situation, his pent-up anger exploded. He quickly apologised for his lack of professionalism but not before he received a promise everything would be on his desk within 48 hours. Quietly satisfied, he headed out. Slowly, slowly, everything was coming together, and soon it would be time to make a move.

DS Hezekiah was making progress, as well. The drugs squad had identified the gang behind the Thursday night drop offs and fully supported a potential raid. So with renewed enthusiasm the two detectives resumed their surveillance, meticulously recording every detail and making sure their preparations were as thorough as possible. There was much to note, from the security arrangements outside the shop, to the timing of the deliveries, but one thing was immediately clear. No way did the takings each day come anywhere close to the amounts that were banked. Yes, there were a few hardy regulars, and hungry families, and the lads in grey tracksuits sometimes had a few chips, but unless prices had increased dramatically, there had to be a lot of dirty cash being laundered through the till.

Somewhere at the heart of this operation was the mysterious Lewis

Sinclair. To all appearances he was simply a cook who after each shift went home to a quiet neighbourhood and lived an ordinary life. Yet his financial records showed he paid no rent, and there was no clue as to how he paid for his fully taxed and insured motorbike, or the BMW parked outside his flat.

And although officially his role was simply that of a fish fryer, it was obvious to Adam and Tunde he was the one who wielded the real authority. When he came out to speak to one of the minions, he immediately commanded their attention. Sometimes he would interrupt a phone conversation by seizing the mobile and apparently giving orders. And even Stan, who owned the business, seemed wary in his presence. Lewis had a physical presence that commanded instant respect and his cold blue eyes could impose discipline with a single look, perhaps accompanied with the odd choice word.

Armed with all this information, the Serious Crimes Unit and the drugs squad met with tactical support on the Friday. It was soon agreed that they would all aim to strike during the delivery the following Thursday evening. That would give a week to arrange everything, and make sure enough evidence was secured as possible.

But as it turned out, this neat timescale was almost completely overturned by a most unexpected turn of events.

Chapter 15

KEVIN SKINNER WAS KNOWN AS Skinny to his mates for obvious reasons and his form tutor was worried about him. Recently he had started turning up late for school, often hungry, and his uniform was sometimes less than clean. He had been in trouble with the police as well, and there was a story he had tried to stab someone. She had tried to speak with his mother, but she barely registered a flicker of interest. According to the word on the street, she had a new man, and they were often away together. His tutor had alerted social services but so far she was still waiting to hear back from them.

It was a grey Monday morning with a biting easterly wind hinting at the coming winter. Several students were off sick, but no-one knew about Skinny. He did not turn up at all that morning and by lunchtime Mrs Delaney was seriously concerned. She had just enough time to call round to his flat. The lights, however, were off and there was no-one at home. But there was a pile of laundry and stacks of dirty crockery in the kitchen. She needed to get back, but she had seen enough.

"Sir," said Blessing McQueen, "we have a problem. Kevin Skinner, the kid we interviewed, is missing."

"Weren't social services supposed to be making an intervention?"

"They haven't assigned a caseworker yet."

Adam wasn't surprised. Whenever he thought about social services, his own lack of resources was as nothing compared to the shortages they were facing. "And I suppose his mother is of no help?"

"She's in Skegness with her boyfriend, and no, she is worse than useless. As for Kevin's dad, no-one knows where he is, and Kevin hasn't, as far as we know, been in touch with him."

Half an hour later DI Will Spencer convened a meeting. "I'd like to know how the hell this happened, but I guess that enquiry will have to wait. We have a missing child. Anyone got any theories as to where he can be? Uniform are at the school and combing social media but so far we don't have a single lead. So give me suggestions, ideas, anything you think might help."

"Start with Paddington Station," said Adam. "OK, this may just be one of my hunches, but consider this: Kevin wants to join the gang in Great Jones Street. He failed the test, and we took him in. So what else can he do? Lewis' mother works at a campsite in Cornwall, and maybe there's a connection. Maybe Kevin is off running an errand, maybe he's heading to the campsite. It's a long shot, I know. But let's at least rule this out."

"I hate it when you have a hunch. OK, Adam, start there. And the rest of you, check out buses, trains, tube, taxis. Kevin must have gone somewhere."

Three hours later Adam's hunch, as so often, proved correct. It was just before seven on the Sunday evening, and there was Kevin nervously entering Paddington Station, but not on his own. He was being guided by Shania McNeil, who led him through to platform 1, where the train to Penzance was waiting. Five minutes later she returned, by now with her headphones on, stopping to buy doughnuts, as if celebrating yet another successful mission.

So where was Kevin heading? Adam spoke to railway staff who confirmed the name of the station closest to Carol Sinclair's campsite.

The train would have stopped there just after eleven. Fortunately, this station had good lighting, and working CCTV. And after a few phone calls, there was the footage Adam needed – Kevin getting off the train, looking utterly lost, only to be greeted by a tall, balding man in his fifties who took his bag and led him to his waiting car.

Adam showed the footage back at the police station.

"So you were right," said DI Spencer.

"Unfortunately I was," said Adam who wished more than anything he had been proved wrong. They then sat looking at the footage from Cornwall for a few minutes in silence until suddenly DI Will Spencer let out a very loud expletive.

"What's up?" asked Adam.

"That man collecting Kevin is none other than Frank Fogarty, the officer once cleared of rape by the testimony of our old friend Carl Carter. Last I heard he was living in Thailand. But now here he is, out and about in Cornwall. How the hell did we miss this?"

"And we have a thirteen year old boy in the company of someone accused of rape. That tells me we act fast, as in yesterday."

"110 percent. I think the first move is to check Kevin really is on the campsite. If he is, that's one question answered. If he's not, we are really in the mire. I'll go make some calls."

An hour later the team were on a video call with their counterparts in the Peninsula Serious Crimes Unit. DI Penhaligon, a thickset Cornishman with a piratical red beard, introduced himself and his team. They had received intelligence that a number of teenagers had arrived on their own at that particular train station over the past few months, and then returned a few days later. The caravan site, however, had not yet been in their sights.

"So," said DI Penhaligon, "do we go in and get the boy immediately?"

DI Spencer deliberated for a moment. "That depends on the evidence you're collecting right now. If he's there and if he's safe, can you hold off until Thursday evening? I don't want news of your raid getting back to Great Jones Street."

"That's a tough call. I need to take it higher up."

DI Spencer nodded. "I'm now going to send you a photo of the man who picked Kevin up. He's called Frank Fogarty. He left the force after being cleared of rape."

"Doesn't ring any bells, but we'll do some digging." One of DI Penhaligon's constables made some notes and then left the call, while someone else handed him a note. "Oh, hot off the press. CCTV from the campsite, that was quick."

At half past eleven last night, there was Kevin Skinner getting out of the car with Carol Sinclair aka Carol Lewis. Frank Fogarty wasn't stopping, however, and another constable duly disappeared to track down the vehicle's movements.

"Well, at least he wasn't alone with our friend Frank," said Adam, and DI Spencer agreed.

"My recommendation," said DI Penhaligon, stroking his beard, "is that we keep the caravan site under surveillance until Thursday evening, collecting evidence, reviewing intelligence and seeing who is coming and going. If we have any reason Kevin is in danger, or if he goes off site, we move in. Otherwise we sit tight until then."

"Is everyone here happy with that?" asked DI Spencer, and without waiting for assent, added, "I will get this plan cleared at our end, and we'll keep in touch."

The call ended, DI Spencer retreated into his office to contact his superiors, while Adam phoned Kevin's mother.

"Is he all right?" she asked, sounding annoyed at the inconvenience of it all, rather than upset.

"He should be back by the end of the week," Adam replied, rather hoping she didn't ask for further explanation.

"So I can stay in Skeggy for a few more days?"

"No, you need to come home so we can talk to you face to face if we need to."

"That boy's nothing but trouble," she said, swearing under her breath.

Adam bit his lip lest he let slip his opinion on her parenting skills and then decided to phone social services, and Kevin's form tutor, Mrs Delaney. The one thing he did not want to happen was for Kevin to go to his life of neglect, even if ultimately that was not his call to make.

By now he should have been back on the evening shift with DS Hezekiah, but there was simply too much to do here. There was a case building against Shania McNeil as well. She had taken the phones from Magnolia House; she had taken Kevin to Paddington Station. Where and when did she meet Kevin? What other errands had she been running? And how was she being paid? He just hoped there were enough resources available to pick her up on Thursday evening as well.

As Adam began to seek answers to these questions, DC Stuart Sawyer was leaving early to celebrate his wedding anniversary.

"Enjoy," said Adam wistfully, "it might be your last free evening for a while."

"Oh, I am well aware of that," said Stuart with a twinkle in his eye, "I intend to make the most of every moment tonight."

And Adam made a mental note to contact Sadie, however late he ended up working.

Chapter 16

THE BITING EASTERLY WIND CARRIED on blowing throughout the week, bringing with it scattered showers and shrouds of grey cloud that still hung heavy on the Thursday evening. Sadie switched her heating on for the first time that autumn, as she held a long phone conversation with her mother, who for the first time hinted at selling the family business.

In her cramped room Jo snuggled up in an extra jumper as she thought about her work, and prepared for her trip to Graz the following day.

In Great Jones Street, Adam was in his usual observation post, but he and Tunde had company. A small team were huddled together, counting the minutes and the hours to the next drugs' delivery. Just out of sight, police vans stuffed with tactically trained officers were waiting for the signal. On the other side of the dividing wall halfway down the street DCI Jones had set up gold command, liaising with colleagues in Cornwall who were keeping tight surveillance on the caravan site, and coordinating raids on Grease's flat and Shania McNeil's flat.

Much debate had taken place about when to strike. At the close of business, the shutters came down on the fish and chip shop, both at the front, and in the loading bay Adam and Tunde had been watching, with the alarm set. The shuttering would only go up when the delivery was being made. That made the outcome of intervention more unpredictable, but no-one wanted to give the gang time to destroy evidence.

Half past ten came. As every night, Stan Collins put out the rubbish, and closed up the shop. He then retired to his second floor flat where it would seem he went straight to bed, while Lewis Sinclair aka Grease waited in the flat below. The grey tracksuited minions melted away in the darkness, some hand in hand with their partners, more of them no doubt waiting for Grease's orders later on that night.

Time passed slowly. Everything was happening exactly as expected, which meant there would now be a long, tedious interval. From time to time someone double checked a detail, while DCI Jones would call in to confirm nothing had changed. Adam said nothing. He remained focused by avoiding any distractions, pushing away the many private thoughts seeking to divert his attention. All that mattered for now was what lay in front of him, and what he expected to happen next.

From time to time, he would gently stretch, or look again at his watch. Eleven. Half past eleven. Midnight. Was there a delay? No, twenty minutes later the hire van from Felixstowe drew up. The shutter opened, Grease came down, greeted the driver, and opened the rear doors. At the same time four young lads appeared from the shadows and began shifting the boxes.

Suddenly there was a tremendous commotion and two police minibuses screeched to a halt, blocking the driver in. The squads of officers, in full body armour, rushed out to apprehend the suspects. The young lads simply froze and were swiftly detained, along with the driver, but in the brief time it took for the officers to dismount, Grease had the presence of mind to rush indoors. But rather than using up valuable seconds bringing the shutter down, he slammed shut the door from the bay to the shop.

"Damn," said Adam, who realised it would take at least a couple of minutes to break down that door. And what would Grease be doing in the meantime?

The answer came soon enough. As soon as the first tactical squad had gained entry they disabled the alarm and raised the shutter in front of the shop so the second squad could join them. What no-one had anticipated, however, was the Molotov cocktail that landed in front of them.

Adam watched on in horror as he realised the officer who had stumbled into the flames was Blessing McQueen. Swiftly two colleagues dragged her away and beat down the flames that were wreathed around her legs. He later counted himself fortunate he could not hear her screams. The only voice, however, in the moment was DCI Jones forcibly demanding the presence of the police helicopter and authorising the deployment of the other emergency services.

Somehow in the lost minutes Grease had made it to the roof, and was making Molotov cocktails out of cooking oil. As the second bottle landed, thankfully missing its aim, a crowd began to form, jeering and uttering threats, while those detained were bundled into police vans. Someone even turned up brandishing a scaffolding pole, and was cheered as he hit one of the vehicles.

"Should we lend a hand?" Adam asked DI Spencer who was sitting next to him. Will had no time to answer, however. The third Molotov cocktail smashed against their window, and for a moment the whole room was alight with flame. "We can't sit here, can we?" Will muttered.

As the detectives emerged into the street, armed police had arrived on scene and detained the pole wielder. The crowd had moved back to a safer distance, but still maintained their chorus of disapproval. Their taunts were drowned out, however, by the approaching helicopter, its powerful searchlight providing clarity to the operation.

The hire van stood with its driver's window smashed in, flanked by the minibuses fore and aft. The police vans in front of them were slowly pulling away, careful not to knock down any onlooker who might be tempted to get in their way. There was just one still parked, where Blessing was being tended by her colleagues, in the protective shelter of the open rear door.

Inside the fish and chip shop, Adam could make out his colleagues methodically moving from floor to floor. Two of them brought Stan Collins out through the loading door. He himself was looking up nervously, wondering what his former charge might do next.

Grease was standing defiantly on the flat roof, with another cocktail in his hand. This one he threw in the direction of the ambulance who braked hard to avoid contact. Then he decided to make a run for it. The roof in each property in the arcade was divided by a low parapet, about three foot high. Grease jumped over the first one with ease, and rushed for the next one, even as the searchlight picked out his every movement.

Only at that moment two armed officers appeared at the top of the fire escape, training their weapons on him. Grease stopped and stood stock still, considering his options. Then in his own time he dropped to his knees, his hands behind his head, as one approached to handcuff him, and the other stood guard.

"Property clear and secured," said DCI Jones. This was the signal for the detectives to move in. DS Pennycome and DS Hezekiah went into the building just as the paramedics were beginning to treat Blessing. Adam knew he had to focus on the task in hand: even so, he mentally paused to pray for her, and to wish for the full force of the law to come down hard on this (expletive deleted) called Lewis Sinclair.

The roof was now a crime scene in its own right, and CSO Jennie and her team arrived to secure evidence just as the drizzle began to set in. At the same time, the two detectives coordinated the search of the property below, starting at the top with Stan Collins' flat. Stan was apparently now single, living a bachelor life, as the surveillance had suspected. There were a couple of bags of cannabis, a little cash, and a mobile, nothing that suggested a major criminal enterprise. On the floor below, the story was very different.

In the living room Grease had laid out the clingfilm, the bags and the disposable gloves to divide up the packages of heroin being delivered that night. In the kitchen were laid out a selection of catering knives, some of which had traces of blood. Whose blood, and whether it was human or piscine, was a task for the lab. Jennie and her team would go over the scene meticulously to see what other evidence could be retrieved. For now, Adam and Tunde bagged up the weapons, along with the mobile phones and SIM cards retrieved from the bedroom, and then proceeded down to the shop to continue their work.

As they continued to investigate freezers and drawers and store cupboards, Adam grimly reflected on the long hours and days that lay ahead. By now it was already five o'clock in the morning, but there was no chance he would be home for breakfast that day, and maybe not even for the next few days. DS Sutton and DC Whittington were collecting more material from Grease's home address, and if that wasn't enough already, DC Watson had apprehended Shania McNeil and was leading the search of her flat in Lilac House. There would be a team meeting at eight o'clock and a short break then, but otherwise the race to present charges to the CPS would be on. At least, Adam reasoned, it shouldn't be too hard to press the case for attempted murder.

It was a similarly long night down in Cornwall. DI Penhaligon found Kevin and a girl from Birmingham living on site, and they were immediately handed over to social services. When Grease's mother, Carol, saw the police officers arriving, she immediately gave herself up. The word was, she was willing to talk to the Serious Crime Unit. Quite when anyone from London would be able to conduct that interview, however, was an open question. Adam had an idea, but that was something he would need to run past DI Spencer.

In the meanwhile, a grey light gradually began to dawn. The drizzle was steady now, and the rain beat down on the tent Jennie had erected to protect the site where a few hours earlier Grease had been throwing his projectiles. The broken bottles down below had now been collected up but there were scorch marks on the tarmac and on the window sill. The ambulance had long gone, but there was no news yet on Blessing's condition. DCI Jones had made it clear there would have to be an independent investigation and lessons learnt review of the night's proceedings.

"More paperwork," said Tunde as they finally emerged into the open air.

"At least all those hours spent together were worth it."

"That reminds me, I have a spare ticket for an MMA fight in a week's time."

"At this rate I will still be pulling overtime," said Adam, who really didn't want to go, "but thanks for the offer."

"Suit yourself. We'll be in touch."

"Sure thing," said Adam who suddenly realised his need for caffeine. He grabbed a large espresso on the way back to the station, and as he did so, mentally readied himself for the task ahead. To get justice for Blessing. To nail Grease once and for all. To honour Niall's memory. To get the support Kevin needed. To untangle the spider's web in Great Jones Street that had grown unchallenged for far too long.

"Right then," he muttered to himself, as he sat down at his computer in a clean shirt, bacon sandwich in hand, "let's do this."

Chapter 17

JUST AS ADAM SAT DOWN at his desk, Jo woke up with another one of her headaches. She had been working all week on some particularly difficult German patents and felt she had done a reasonably good job on them, bearing in mind the tight deadline. Her manager hadn't even bothered to respond to all the work she had sent her. Jo already suspected the firm was trying to find ways of getting her to quit, and she longed for a working environment where her work was valued. She had gone home on Friday frustrated and nearly tripped over the empty packing cases her new neighbours had left outside her door. Unlike her brother, however, Jo internalised her anger and that usually meant lost sleep and pounding headaches. As she hauled herself out of bed, she was almost tempted to call her visit off and crawl back under the covers. But no, she owed this visit to the memory of Uncle David, and besides, she needed the break from her routine.

However, she was also going to visit someone she had never met before and give them a total surprise. Jo packed nervously, trying to imagine what might be appropriate. She settled on a long, smart skirt and a fairly plain blouse, to convey some air of respectability. Or maybe something else? She took some paracetamol and codeine, washed down with gin, as it was hard to think straight. But since no alternative presented itself, she carried on packing and then set off to the nearest tube station.

It was only as she arrived that Jo realised she had forgotten to have any breakfast. She had planned to leave herself plenty of time at Heathrow but with the overcrowding and inevitable delays, time was tighter than she had planned. By now she was hot and bothered, and her headache was attempting a comeback. She grabbed an utterly unforgettable meal somewhere, and soldiered on through long queues, down long corridors, and past confused and bewildered stragglers until finally she found her plane, plugged in her earphones and allowed herself to breathe.

By contrast her arrival in Graz could hardly have been easier. The airport was a small, compact international terminal that easily connected with a train which took her effortlessly into the city. From what she saw out of the window, it was a modern well laid out conurbation that invited further exploration. To her right lay a cemetery and Jo wondered if that was where Erwald Bach was buried. She thought of the letters she had read and Claudia's decision to stay with him, even against the desires of her heart. Was Claudia now happy and would she be breaking her happiness? For Jo, her knowledge of such matters came only from the books she had read. She had no real experience of loving or being loved, except by her own family, and she rarely had the energy to consider what might be missing from her life.

At the station she found a polite, well-groomed taxi driver who seemed astonished that an English girl could speak such good German. Jo smiled and felt Uncle David would have been proud of her. She sensed he wouldn't have minded paying for her hotel, either. She let the taxi driver take her suitcase into the reception, and picked up the key to her room. She had intended to have a meal and then go exploring, but after she had eaten, she suddenly felt utterly exhausted and went straight to bed.

Jo woke up with a start at about four, after anxious dreams about missed deadlines, and failing to recognise the most basic words, and turning up for work in her pyjamas. She needed to do something. She began searching for possible alternative jobs, but found very little. She looked at some creative writing courses, which had always been one of her ambitions, and wondered how on earth she could ever afford it. She went onto Facebook but only found herself annoyed by the ignorance and superficiality she found there. In the end she downloaded an irritatingly addictive game which she played until she was ready to go back to sleep. Jo sensed there was an emptiness she was trying to fill, but couldn't work out how else to deal with it.

Jo finally surfaced again about ten. She ran herself a long, deep bath, feeling the need to be clean from all the dirt and grime of the daily grind that was so getting her down, and then she checked her emails. Predictably there was one from her manager, not commenting on her work, but offering either redundancy or a freelance contract. Jo sighed. She wished she could talk the situation over with her parents but knew they would only tell her to find a proper job, like Sally. And it would be no use asking for money. She knew they were helping Sally pay her rent, even though her dad kept telling her how money ain't what it used to be.

Brooding on the unfairness of it all, Jo got dressed in her carefully planned outfit, went outside and found a coffee shop where she discovered the delights of a Krapfen, lightly coated in icing sugar and filled with apricot jam. Perhaps, she thought, the day wouldn't be so bad after all. Then she made her way up the Schlossberg, all the while thinking of Claudia's letters as she made her way up the steep steps. The view from there truly was spectacular, over the red tiled rooftops to the skyline beyond, and in the distance rolling hills. She found an ice cream in the shadow of the clock tower and sat on a bench, trying to imagine what Claudia and David must have felt, reunited so fleetingly after so many years apart, no doubt drawing a bittersweet comparison between past and present.

Jo finished her ice cream thoughtfully and then checked on the best way to get to Eggenberg. It was by now one o'clock and Jo knew she couldn't put the moment off any longer. She caught a bus, and made sure she knew where to get off. By now she was getting nervous, and her headache once again threatened to erupt. But as she made her way to the neat, whitewashed house, she asked herself what was the worst that could happen.

There was a path to the front door lined with rosebushes, which were now neatly pruned skeletons, carefully covered to protect from the coming frosts. There was no sign of movement behind the fastidiously pretty net curtains. Jo was very conscious of the sound of her footsteps. She approached the door, hesitated then resolutely pulled the doorbell.

An immaculately dressed lady, carefully made up, answered the door. She opened it only slightly, and peered round it with sharp, intelligent eyes that asked Jo a direct question.

"Gruess Gott," said Jo, composing herself.

"Gruess Gott," replied Claudia in a neutral tone, still asking the same question with her eyes.

"Ich heisse Jo Pennycome," replied Jo, daring to look straight at her.

Jo noted the look of surprise on Claudia's face and waited for the door to open further. But instead Claudia sadly shook her head and shut it firmly in her face.

Jo stood there for the moment, wondering what to do. Eventually she fished a pen and paper out of her rucksack, wrote down her phone number and address, and put it through Claudia's door, explaining she was in Graz until Wednesday. Suddenly a long afternoon presented itself, and she was unexpectedly free.

She had read about a local castle and its gardens, and decided to walk there. It was a bright autumn afternoon where the sunlight was still warm and clear. On the way she passed an international school and for a moment thought about seeing if they had any vacancies. But then she reminded herself of her resolution never to teach, and the experiences others had told of that profession, and she decided she was not desperate enough to go down that route.

The gardens were even more impressive than she had read about. They had been laid out in the English style and Jo loved simply exploring the grounds. The trees were turning a rich palette of colours, and Jo pretended she was a little girl again walking through the leaves. She eventually ended up in the planetary garden with its strange assortment of geometric patterns, and she tried to guess which pattern represented which planet. She sat there a while reading a small poetry book she had brought with her from England until she decided it was time to go back to the hotel.

Jo then wondered what to do next. All she could do, she reasoned, was wait. Darkness was fast drawing in, so she went to the dining room and ordered a meal. Then she went back to her room, and having found the minibar, settled down to watch a film. The hours passed slowly. She was just changing into pyjamas when her phone rang in her hotel room. "Am I speaking Jo Pennycome?" asked a deep voice in broken English. Jo responded fluently in German, and established the caller's identity as Thomas Bach. They agreed to meet for lunch the next day, and Jo found it hard to contain a note of excitement. She had been afraid of returning home to England with no news, with questions unanswered. But now she had every reason to hope those fears had been allayed. She immediately texted Adam and Sadie, and went to bed in a far happier frame of mind.

The following morning in Graz was suddenly a lot colder, and as if from nowhere the first few flakes of snow lay on the ground. Jo reminded herself that so far from the sea the weather could turn suddenly. The layers she had brought with her were inadequate, so she spent the morning looking for a suitable coat she could afford. Eventually her desire for warmth and her budget were satisfied, but there was still another hour to go. She snuggled in the corner of a coffee shop, reading the local news on her phone, while at the same time watching the minutes go by.

Fifteen minutes to go, Jo paid her bill and made her way to the restaurant. She explained to an officious waiter that she was expecting someone, and she began her vigil. Ten, fifteen, twenty minutes went by. She thought of Claudia waiting for David at the station all those years ago. And then Thomas Bach came. Jo recognised him at once, an older, fatter and shorter version of her brother, with the same dark eyes, and strong chin, and upright stance. He kissed Jo lightly on the cheek.

"You could almost pass for my daughter," he said.

"Wait until you see the rest of my family." Jo showed him a picture of the last Pennycome family gathering.

"Ach, I looked like your brother ten years ago. Come, let us eat and drink, and tell strange stories."

Thomas led Jo to a table he had booked in a quiet corner, and pulled out her chair for her. To Jo's relief, Thomas made it quite clear he was paying – Jo had been worrying how to afford both a coat and the meal. Thomas went through the menu with her, and gave his opinion of the dishes worth having. In the end both of them settled on a light soup followed by liver dumplings. They chatted cordially until the food came. Then Jo asked directly, "Did you ever suspect Erwald was not your real father?"

"Ach, ja. From an early age I never felt a real connection with him. Erwald was always so formal. He always wanted rules to obey in everything, and he expected me to follow these rules as well. If he had a heart, he hid it from me and my mother, and I asked myself how they ever married. When I was twelve, I dared to ask Mother that same question directly. She replied that she had nothing and Erwald offered her something. I did not hear love in her answer."

"And did she ever tell you who your real father was?"

"I was curious, of course, but I could never ask that question directly while Erwald was alive. If I did, I could have destroyed their marriage and Father, as I called him, could be so cruel. But a few weeks after the funeral, I did ask who my real father was. Mother said it was in the past, and my father couldn't now be found. I think she wanted to leave the past in the past, and I had to respect her decision."

"Your father was my Great-Uncle David," said Jo. "I have brought some letters for you to read. I wasn't sure whether to tell Claudia he kept them until the end of his life, but I think you should read them."

Thomas' eyes watched with surprise as Jo handed the precious folder of his mother's correspondence. As he began to read, he gently laid the spoon on the table. His eyes by now were filling with tears, and Jo gently laid her hand on his.

"And your great-uncle never married?" asked Thomas when he finished reading.

"No," said Jo, "we only knew him as a kindly old man who lived alone. He never told of the woman he loved."

There was a moment's silence as Thomas and Jo both reflected on the secrets of the past. Then the officious waiter noticed neither of them were eating and came to ask if the food pleased them. Thomas waved him away, like a man shooing away a fly.

"You know," he said finally, "I am so glad Erwald was not my father. After he died, it transpired that he was an orderly at the Liebenau camp here in Graz."

"I have never heard of this camp," replied Jo, surprised.

"It was a transit camp for Hungarian Jews to the south of the city. We Grazer have tended to forget about it, as so much of our past."

"There seems a certain irony that your real father was a man who served in the army that liberated the city."

"Exactly. I am thinking now how to tell all this story to my wife and my daughter. This seems to me a story that must not be forgotten again. But come, let us drink to David Pennycome, and let us eat in his honour."

Thomas and Jo touched glasses, and they began to tell each other of their families. Thomas had married a woman whose grandparents had fled Hungary in 1956, the same journey, he explained, that Claudia and her mother had made twelve years previously. They now had a ten year old daughter Sonja who hoped one day to be a doctor. And then Jo talked about Sally and her three children, and about Adam, without, however, being clear whether she should mention Sadie. And so the conversation went on, until after nearly three hours Thomas said he had to go and pick Sonja up from school. Before he left, he gave the waiter something useful to do by asking him to photograph them on their phones. Jo wanted to give Thomas the letters, but he declined, stating that Mother might still want to destroy them. Then he kissed Jo again and disappeared out into the snow.

Jo, however, wasn't so ready to go. She ordered a coffee and then proceeded to send the photos to Adam and Sadie. She realised that in this moment she felt suddenly and wonderfully alive, and putting her coat back on, she went outside, with a great sense of warmth in her heart. If there was a God, thought Jo, he had surely smiled on this day.

Chapter 18

AROUND THE TIME JO WAS sitting down to lunch with her cousin once removed, Adam finally arrived home. The main suspects, Lewis Sinclair, Stan Collins and Shania McNeil, had been charged and remanded, after the obligatory no comment interviews. Stan had prepared a statement denying direct involvement in the events of Thursday evening, but neither Lewis nor Shania offered any defence.

There was a cold impassivity in Lewis' demeanour that had unsettled Adam. He had been prepared to offer some sympathy to a young man who had been brought up in a criminal environment, but Lewis' body language showed he did not deal in the currency of kindness. He stared straight ahead, cracking his knuckles from time to time, completely ignoring the careworn duty solicitor who was making copious notes.

But now Lewis had been transferred out of the police station. Any further charges would be brought when finally forensics had the results. There would be more arrests later in the week, when the tech guys had gone through all the phones collected, and the drugs squad were closing in on those further up the supply chain. For now there was a brief lull, the eye of the storm as DC Sawyer put it, and Adam intended to take full advantage.

Adam cooked his first proper meal for days, spaghetti and

meatballs, had a long shower and then settled into a deep sleep, for once untroubled by nightmares or thoughts of Sadie. He woke with a start, however, when his alarm went off at seven o'clock that evening, and wished for a moment he could roll over and resume his slumbers.

With DI Spencer's agreement he drove down to Little Netherworthy Lodge in an official unmarked vehicle. It was a relatively easy journey with light traffic. The drizzle of the past week had cleared and once in the countryside Adam could see a full moon lighting his way.

But Adam's thoughts were only on what lay ahead. Rationally, he told himself it made no difference that a crime had been committed in the house all those years ago, or that his fellow officers had searched the whole property from top to bottom. Yet even so, as he swung through the gates, a little before midnight, he could sense a certain amount of apprehension.

Derek had left some milk, bread and eggs in the fridge, and turned the heating on low. Adam was used to entering strange buildings in complete darkness but somehow this time it was different. Carefully and thoroughly he went through every room, not quite sure what he expected to find. Fortunately, DI Gregory's team had gone to great lengths to put everything back as far as possible, and there was very little missing or out of place.

It was the silence, however, that got to Adam. He turned on the radio as he cooked his eggs, and wondered what Sadie would make of the garden now. From the pictures he had seen, the whole site had been stripped and excavated, but he would find out more in the morning. He knew that he would find it impossible to sleep, so after his supper, he once more went for a run, pounding the quiet lanes, concentrating on the physical sensation of movement, and contemplating the day ahead.

But first on that Monday morning Adam had a visitor. He was not by nature superstitious, and he could not really explain why he had invited the vicar James round. But he reasoned there was no harm in the property being blessed, and indeed it might do some good.

So they sat down with their mug of tea, and Adam was again struck by the simplicity of the prayers: for the family of the man who had been murdered, for the murderer to recognise the evil he had done, for those who had discovered the body and the police in their work, and for the house to be a place of love, security and peace. And as he prayed, Adam suddenly knew with complete certainty this was where he wanted to live, if at all possible with Sadie.

"Thank you," said Adam, who found himself deeply moved.

"You are very welcome, and thank you for asking me."

They chatted briefly for a while and then as James left, he gave Adam a small wooden holding cross. "I don't know about all the stuff you deal with, but some of it must be pretty unpleasant. Here's something you can take with you."

Adam shut the door and took a deep breath. Most of the time he could keep his emotions in check without any difficulty but maybe the strain of the past weeks was catching up with him. At least that was what he told himself, although he knew it was something more.

He then drove to the solicitors where Christopher Brunt was expecting him. But before he got out of the car, he sent a long email to Sadie expressing his great desire to meet. He realised that even in the middle of October she was up to her eyes in Christmas orders, yet even so he prayed he would receive a reply soon.

"You look like a man with much on your mind," said Christopher in a genial, avuncular style. "Well, this shouldn't take long. A few forms to sign and probate should be sorted soon."

Adam penned his signature and returned the paperwork. "Just one question," continued Christopher, "do you think the Granada has any probate value? Or at least is worth more than it costs to fix it?"

Adam considered his answer for a moment and then a thought suddenly hit him. "I'm sorry," he said, "but there's someone I need to phone urgently."

"I am sure you have much urgent business in your line of work," said Christopher stiffly, "I will be in touch again as and when."

Out in the car park Adam rang DI Gregory who for once was at his desk.

"Not much to report," said DI Gregory, "with very little forensic evidence we are only building the case against Billy Hurst very slowly."

"I may be able to help."

"Not if you've been freelancing," DI Gregory replied curtly.

"Here's the thing. Before we came across Timmy Taylor I had my great-uncle's Ford Granada taken away for restoration. I believe David let his tenants use his cars."

"Now you tell me," sighed DI Gregory, "so give me the name of the garage."

Adam duly obliged.

"Thank you, and by the way, great work on that drugs raid."

"I'm off to see DI Penhaligon now."

"Our very own Cornish pirate. Enjoy. And oh – and this is strictly off the record – there may be an opening down this way you may be interested in about April time next year."

"I will bear that in mind," said Adam smiling. As he ended the call, he happened to notice the text from his sister he had somehow missed. "Well done, sis," he said to himself. Suddenly the many fragments of his life were coming together, and he felt unusually optimistic about the future.

His good mood continued as he arrived in the county of his ancestors. True to type, DI Penhaligon met him, wearing long black boots, faded jeans, and a striped sweater, partly obscured by his long rust coloured beard. "Carol's in protective custody," he explained. "When you meet her, you'll understand why."

Greg Penhaligon then led him into an interview room where Grease's mother was sitting. She was a tall, fair woman with deep furrows on her forehead, and large, nervous blue eyes, accented by unnaturally bright mascara.

"This is DS Pennycome from the Thames Serious Crimes' Unit."

"I always knew I would end up talking to one of the boys there. Carl often mentioned the unit, and the people he knew there."

"I am sure he did," said Adam, looking at her full in the face and seeing a woman borne down by many cares. "So tell me about your relationship with Carl Carter."

"Let's see now. I must have met him about 25 years ago. I had just survived a shit marriage (excuse my French) when this handsome, gorgeous looking young policeman came into my life. I couldn't believe my luck, and as it turned out, it was too good to be true."

"Go on."

"Carl was always ambitious. Said he always wanted the very best for me, and that his policeman's pay was never enough. So he started what he called "dabbling", making deals, building up his own little business that gradually grew bigger and bigger. I didn't want to know what he was doing, and he didn't tell me. At first I liked the designer gear he bought me but gradually I felt more and more uncomfortable."

"Where does Stan Collins fit into all this?"

"Oh, they were stepbrothers. Stan never had it in him to be a criminal mastermind. He only really wanted to run a chippy. But Carl saw an opportunity, and when he had an idea, you went along with what he said."

"I can imagine. So here you are living with Carl, bringing up Lewis, maybe uncomfortable about what's happening, but still with things looking up. What made you leave?"

Carol hesitated for a moment and looked at him quizzically. "Would you say I was mad if I said God spoke to me?" Adam shook his head. After all that had happened that day, he was hardly in a position to question her faith.

"I started going to church with Gloria McNeil, Stan's girlfriend at the time. I was the only white woman there, but no-one seemed to mind. One Sunday I had this conviction I needed to break free. I believe to this day it was the Holy Spirit speaking to me."

"Yet you left Lewis behind."

"Carl had already brainwashed him. Even aged eight he was running small errands, if you know what I mean. I prayed hard and hoped Stan and Gloria would look after him. Carl was never going to be a single parent, as you can probably tell."

"Did you ever meet Shania?"

"Spoilt little child who always got her own way. I expect she's mixed up in all this."

"So you found God. The Holy Spirit spoke to you, and you started a new life in Cornwall. Yet here we are today, in a police cell, and you are facing charges of child trafficking."

Carol looked at him and then genuinely broke down in tears. "I am so sorry," she said, as her mascara ran onto the tissues. "Sometimes I think my whole life has been one big screw up."

"I am not here to show pity," said Adam, with professional detachment, "but I may be able to help if you can give some kind of explanation."

"I saw Lewis several times as he grew up. He used to come down here on holiday with Stan and Gloria, before they split up. I could see he was turning into his father, not just in how he looked, but how he behaved. Never said he loved me, always expected me to do as he wanted."

At that point, the interview was briefly paused as mugs of tea were brought in, for which everyone was grateful. Adam's hand ached from the sheer amount of writing and his pen was starting to run out.

Carol composed herself, took a long slurp and continued. "Then about three years ago Lewis turned up out of the blue. He said dad was retiring and handing over the business to him. I asked him why he was telling me this. He said he had an idea, and I knew exactly what that meant. Whatever he was about to tell me, I had to go along with."

"And what if you didn't?"

The momentary look of terror told Adam all he needed to know. "No-one who wants to live ever says no," replied Carol in a trembling voice. "That's how I ended up housing those kids."

"I have a list of their names," added DI Penhaligon, "Carol kept a secret record."

"I am sure that is useful," said Adam, who understood the bravery behind that action. "For the record, did you know why the children were there, and what they were doing?"

"Of course. They were supplying drugs."

"Were you directly involved in the supply of drugs?"

"No," said Carol in a note of panic. "I knew this was wrong, all wrong – may Christ forgive me – but I did what I could. I fed the kids, I made sure they were comfortable. One or two even thanked me."

The compassionate face of county lines, thought Adam cynically.

"I don't want to repeat DI Penhaligon's questioning, but one final thing. What is your relationship with Frank Fogarty?"

"Who? I have never heard of him."

"The man who picked Kevin Skinner up from the station."

"Oh, is that his real name? I always knew him as Shane Stephens."

Adam paused for a moment. So that was the person behind the holding company that owned Lewis Sinclair's flat. It was all beginning to make sense now.

"How long have you known Shane Stephens?"

"I would hardly say I know him. Your colleague will be able to confirm I don't have his contact details. He first started turning up when Lewis took over the business. He seemed to come and go as he pleased. I sensed he was the one person Lewis looked up to. I wouldn't be surprised if he was one of Carl's gang."

Adam tried to keep a neutral expression, but he couldn't at that moment help thinking about the rape trial. "Do you know where Frank, I mean Shane, used to stay?"

"He never said anything much about himself. I think he had a boat, or yacht, but I can't give any details."

"We are starting to make enquiries," explained DI Penhaligon.

"Do you know where he is now?"

Carol shook her head. "Last thing he said to me he was going away on business for a while."

Later on, when the interview had been concluded, Greg turned to Adam and said, "I love it when canaries sing."

"Look after her. We need her alive," replied Adam grimly.

"Oh, we will," said Greg. "Look, it's half past six now, and I know a great pub not far from here that's famous for its pies."

Adam hesitated. He was anxious to get back and share the intelligence, but he needed sustenance for the journey, and besides here was someone who might one day become his colleague.

"Go on, then. But I can't stay long."

"That's the spirit. I can always recognise a fellow Cornishman when I see one."

Chapter 19

IT WAS NOT UNTIL WEDNESDAY morning that Sadie replied to Adam's email. She had, of course, been working flat out, and soon she would have to make a decision about expanding the business. So she had spent the last few evenings, with her headphones on, poring over spreadsheets. But as she unlocked the unit in the gloom of a cold, drizzly dawn she finally admitted to herself she was only trying to block out the most important decision of all.

She remained huddled in her duffel coat while the heater in the small back office struggled into life, and opened up her laptop. As she thought about what to say, she fingered her cross and prayed silently. In the end, she settled on simply offering a date. She could pour out her heart in an email, but she was wise enough to know secrets such as she bore could only be shared face to face.

Now there was nothing more to do than wait. That Adam still wanted her after all this time was, she acknowledged, nothing short of a miracle and however painful, she needed to make nothing less than a full and honest disclosure. She sighed and put on the kettle. A dose of caffeine and a backlog of orders was exactly what she needed to kick-start the day.

But as she piled into the day's business she noticed a couple of personal messages lurking in her inbox amid all the trade correspondence. One was, unusually, from her mother. It was addressed to her and her brother Kevin to officially announce that Christmas 2019 would be the final season for the hotel. After much discussion she and their father had decided to market it in the early spring as a going concern.

Sadie smiled. She could never imagine her mother retiring. Even when she was young, it was her father who usually picked her up from school, took her to training, attended parents' evening. Her mother only really took a break in January when the hotel closed for two weeks, and she and Kevin would put up the tree and hang the decorations just as everyone else was putting them down. So would her parents do now? There was no clue in the message, but if Sadie knew anything her father was even now gently, patiently, persuading her mother to take a break.

There was also an email from Jo. She had spent her last evening in Graz with Thomas Bach and his family, and Sadie was pleased Jo was looking so relaxed and happy. There was a picture of her with her arms around Sonja who could almost have been mistaken for her little sister, and there could be no doubt this was a gathering of the Pennycome clan. Only Thomas' wife, Anna, stood out, with her fair, light hair and sparkling blue eyes, but as Jo explained, she was expecting early next year and very much hoping her next child would take after her.

As Sadie looked at the photos, it suddenly felt very important to her to be part of this family one day. There was, however, on this dull, grey morning no immediate remedy for her aching heart. So, with a sigh, she brewed her tea, took off her coat and attended to the first order of the day, with a forced, steely determination.

Adam of course had received the same email from his sister. He was proud of how well Jo had accomplished her mission, and deliberately told her so, but he couldn't help being concerned with her immediate future. He had an idea forming in the back of his mind, but he had no opportunity to take it further that day. As he turned into the prison courtyard, he said to DC Stuart Sawyer, "Long day of interviews ahead."

"Indeed. But as this is likely to be my last major case, let's make sure we do a proper job."

Stan Collins was already waiting for them as they passed into the interview room. He cut a lonely, dejected figure and Adam wondered if he was ill. His faded navy sweatshirt hung loosely about him, and his pale cheeks were drawn and haggard. But Adam was not here to offer sympathy. There was a jigsaw here that needed putting together, and Carol had provided the first pieces.

"So, tell us about your relationship with Carl Carter."

"He was my younger brother. But I expect you've worked that out by now."

"I think my colleague was talking about your business relationship," Stuart interjected.

Stan sighed deeply. "It was all his idea. I thought it would be a nice little earner on the side, if you know what I mean. I never imagined..." But at this point his thin, frail voice tailed off.

Adam let the silence hang for a while and looked straight at Stan, who, however, kept his attention fixed on the worn, wobbly table beneath him.

"And what did the business become?"

"No comment," said Stan softly.

"Well, let's talk about your nice little earner, as you put it. Carl built up the business, you went along with it, and then Carl retired. But you had already made sure there was a successor in place. You had taken on Lewis as one of your own, you let him work in your fish and chip shop."

"I had no choice!"

"When you take responsibility for an eight year old child, I suggest you have plenty of choices."

"You don't understand."

"So help me. I need to know how this drug ring operated for so many years right under our noses."

"When Carl made up his mind to do something, you had to go along. Do I need to say more?" Stan for a moment looked straight back at Adam with sad, slightly bloodshot blue eyes. "And it wasn't just Carl. It was his mates as well."

"Such as Frank Fogarty?"

"No comment."

"And where does Shania fit into all this?"

"Oh, Carl had her under his spell, as well. She was his little errand girl."

"Tell me about the errand Shania ran on the night Niall O'connor died."

"I don't know nothing. You'll have to ask Lewis."

"Was Lewis working in the shop that night?"

"No comment."

"And what about Kevin Skinner?"

"Who?"

"Lewis never mentioned him?"

"No comment."

"So," said Stuart, with a well-planned intervention, "here you are running your fish and chip shop. You are getting paid by your brother to do what? To turn a blind eye? To launder dirty money through the till?"

"We have been through your accounts," added Adam. "For a shop of your size, you employ a lot of staff. We are slowly tracking them down, but a few are proving quite hard to find."

"I paid my taxes," said Stan.

"Of course you did. The last thing you wanted was HMRC snooping around. We'll be coming back to you with a complete list of names once we have been back to the beginning. We intend to be thorough."

"But that's only the beginning," added Stuart. "We're also very keen to track down the lads who were hanging around outside."

"They were a f***ing nuisance. I told Lewis I wanted them gone."

"And how did Lewis react?"

"He told me he liked a good laugh," said Stan with a touch of bitterness.

"We're getting the picture," said Adam, "so talk to us about Thursday nights."

"That's when I do a special offer on curried chicken."

"You know that isn't what I'm talking about."

"You know I was in my flat when your boys came knocking."

"We also know that's when you received a call from the Felixstowe area."

"No comment," said Stan tersely.

"Was this to confirm the heroin had arrived safely? Or to make arrangements for the following week?"

"No comment."

"Those calls follow a pattern," and here Adam produced a piece of paper from his briefcase. "Every Thursday night, a phone call from the Felixstowe area. Different number each time, same approximate location. That piece of evidence alone tells me you were far more involved than you are letting on."

"When you run your own business," added Stuart, "you need to be organised, you need to handle paperwork. And I was impressed by the quality of your accounts. Especially when you seemed to do them yourself."

"I think I have said quite enough already," said Stan quietly, and he suddenly looked drained.

As the warder led Stan away, Adam turned to Stuart, "I don't think any jury is going to buy the innocent victim defence."

"Agreed. Now let's see what Lewis has to say for himself."

Lewis Sinclair was housed in a separate unit, about an hour's drive away, along crowded dual carriageways flanked by dreary industrial estates and boarded up shopping centres. In the drizzle of late October, Adam had to confess he was finding the appeal of Little Netherworthy Lodge growing ever stronger, or at least life there with Sadie.

But there was no time to daydream. Again, Lewis Sinclair was waiting for them, but his demeanour could not have been more different to that of his stepfather. He was leaning slightly forward, in a crisp white tee shirt that emphasised his powerful biceps, and drew attention to the lion tattooed down his right arm.

Adam and Stuart spent the best part of three hours presenting the facts of the case against him. Every time he replied with the same cold, clear answer, "No comment." From time to time he would crack his knuckles or flex said biceps. Adam and Stuart had expected this response, and the only wonder was how such a dangerous individual had escaped attention for so long – although they both knew the answer.

It was late afternoon by the time the interview was done. But just before it was over, Adam suddenly switched tack.

"So let's talk about your mother."

"No comment."

"Why did she leave you behind when you were eight years old?"

"No comment."

"It must have been hard for you to lose her. Did it make you angry or sad?"

"No comment." Lewis kept the same even tone throughout which unnerved Adam. Was his mother really a matter of indifference or was he simply incapable of emotion?

"Did you try to keep in touch?"

"No comment."

"We know you visited her three years ago. Did you threaten her? Or was she too scared to refuse your proposal?"

"No comment."

"This is your own mother we are talking about. You suddenly turn up after many years and use her for your county lines operation. From your responses it sounds like you treated her as just another pawn in your game. Just like Niall O'connor. Just like Kevin Skinner. Just like almost anyone you came into contact with. She was just someone to be used as you saw fit."

"You've been talking to her, haven't you?" said Lewis.

"Finally," said Adam with a note of triumph, "we get a complete sentence. But let me be clear, in this interview I ask the questions."

Lewis said nothing, but retained the same erect composure. "Of course," added Stuart, "if she was a threat, you would know how to deal with her. That much has become all too clear from our investigations."

Lewis just smiled and cracked his knuckles once more, and Adam made a mental note to review Carol's security arrangements. Then he noted the time, stopped the tape and concluded the investigation.

"In all my years," said Stuart afterwards, "I have rarely seen a piece of work like Lewis."

"But I am sure Carl was proud of him."

"Yes," agreed Stuart, "that explains a lot."

They drove on in the gathering darkness back to the station. Adam knew there was a good couple of hours' of paperwork ahead of him. It was all part and parcel of doing a proper job and he was more determined than ever to see Lewis Sinclair locked away for a very long time. But first, he needed to run a small errand of his own.

The hospital where Blessing was being treated lay not far from the station. Adam still felt a sense of guilt at what had happened to her, even though he kept telling himself this guilt was irrational, and he felt duty bound to visit.

She was asleep when he found her, and Adam noted how exhausted she seemed, no doubt racked by the pain of her injuries. She was connected to a morphine drip, and her leg was carefully wrapped in burn dressings. And next to her, her father Victor was keeping a silent vigil, his hands clasped in wordless prayer, his head bowed onto the edge of the bed.

Adam suddenly realised he didn't belong there. As Victor turned to face him with a weary, questioning expression, he mumbled an apology and handed over the card he had brought. Then he headed back to the station, to file his reports and to dream that possibly, just possibly there was an email from Sadie waiting for him when he got home.

Chapter 20

AT ADAM'S SUGGESTION, JO MOVED into Lower Netherworthy Lodge just as the clocks went back. She could no longer afford to live in London, even in a shared house, and the lodge was going to stand empty at least to the middle of next year, when Adam was reckoning to get his transfer.

Jo had never lived in such a quiet, peaceful place before, but unlike her brother, she soon adapted to the overwhelming sense of solitude. She had up until this point always lived anonymously in crowds, complying and conforming where necessary, but at the same time increasingly wishing to stand apart. Now, she hoped, that wish was about to be fulfilled, and she clung onto the dream that life at the lodge might finally enable her to start writing as she had always wanted.

But first she had to earn a living, and save up to get a place of her own. It was true she had her freelance work, but those earnings only went so far, and she was never very sure when the next assignment would come her way. So one dark morning she walked up the lane with her headtorch, braved the verge of the main road and enquired at the garden centre whether there was any work. The cafe was already closed for the winter, but the seasonal workers had gone home, and there were some hours going in the farmshop, frequented by passing travellers and a loyal band of residents from the local villages.

Jo therefore soon settled into a routine and rhythm, far less hurried and stressful than in the capital, but also, she realised, in many ways far more natural. There were still the long evenings to contend with, of course, and in a way Jo missed the sound of the traffic, the random snatches of music from open car windows, the chatter of pedestrians talking into their phones. She also missed hopping on a bus to see Sally and the children, perhaps letting her sister cut and style her hair, perhaps playing games with her nephew and nieces, who were all growing up so fast.

But she found ways of occupying herself. She was getting to know her recently discovered Austrian family, and she chatted regularly with Sonja who wanted help improving her English. There was also her niece Lucy, about the same age as Sonja, who much to Sally's puzzlement was developing an insatiable appetite for books, exactly like the ten year old Jo. And then there was Sadie. Jo couldn't be sure, but from all the conversations with her, she felt certain her brother and Sadie would sooner or later get together. The only puzzle was why this hadn't happened before now, but Jo was the first to admit she was no expert in relationships, and there were some things that she just couldn't explain.

Even so, there were times, especially at the weekends, when the silence hung heavy, and Jo found herself in a particularly listless mood. That is when she would open a bottle or two of wine from the farmshop, run a long bath, and hopefully get out again before she drifted into a deep, dreamless sleep. Then the next morning she would wake up, and scold herself for behaving like her mother, whom, in her teenage years, she had many a time found passed out on the bathroom floor.

One thing Adam did not know was that, when his mother was drunk, she would send long messages to Jo and Sally complaining how unhappy she was, and how she wished she had never moved to Spain. She rarely remembered sending these messages and refused point blank to discuss them when sober. That explained why before opening a bottle of wine, Jo would switch off her phone. As far as she knew, her drinking was her secret and she fully intended it to stay that way.

There were times, however, when the bottle stayed unopened, at least for that evening. Then Jo would lie on the bed listening to the rain falling, or the wind rushing through the trees, or even occasionally the barking of a fox, or the call of an owl. She had never really encountered the raw power of weather before, or the wildness of nature, and she began to understand in a new way the poetry she had always loved and treasured.

She was listening to one particularly violent storm towards the end of the month, when suddenly she heard a tremendous crack, followed by the snap of branches and the mighty rustling of leaves. She instantly realised a tree must have blown over in the copse behind the lodge, but in the total darkness of the countryside there was nothing she could do.

With an almost childish sense of anticipation, Jo waited for first light, only dozing fitfully from time to time and having vivid, but unpleasant dreams. And when she drew back the curtains, her suspicions were confirmed. Beyond the garden, now bare and lifeless after the police excavations, the skeleton of an oak tree was resting precariously on top of the laurel hedge.

Jo dressed up warmly to investigate. The storm had passed, but there was still a chill drizzle on the breeze. She walked out of the lodge, then a little way up the driveway to the flats, and inspected the large root ball that had toppled over and left a large gaping wound in the ground. It was an impressive sight, and she began to wonder how she might describe the scene in that first, elusive novel.

It was as the first sentences were forming that she noticed something blue sticking out from the corner of the hole. She approached it cautiously, suddenly remembering the skull under the patio. Most of the time she had managed to shut that discovery out of her mind, and avoid thinking how or why the terrible crime had been committed. But here obviously was a suitcase and she could think of no good reason why anyone would want to bury it, unless they had something to conceal.

Jo ran back into the house and immediately rang Adam. He listened to her excited tones and then sighed deeply. "Jo, you know I can't touch this. This is not my investigation, and I don't want, I really don't want to spend a day in court being taken apart by a defence solicitor."

Jo felt deflated. As usual her elder brother was talking perfect sense, but she still wished he occasionally sounded a little more human. "So what do I do?"

"Ring DI Gregory," he said, unexpectedly kindly, "I have his direct number here."

As it happened, Adam was just about to see Shania McNeil and her solicitor. The request for a meeting had come out of the blue, and Adam wondered quite what lay in store. The long, protracted investigation was constantly revealing new information and he was working flat out to keep on top of developments, conscious all the while of the overtime he was accruing.

The first time Adam had interviewed Shania, she had been almost as defiant as Lewis, with her bold "No comment," answers. But now something had changed. Fidgety and nervous, she avoided any eye contact at all as Adam walked into the room of the prison where she was being held on remand.

"My client would like me to read the statement she has written," announced her solicitor, a lady called Patience Ojo, who was dressed in purple, with flame red hair spilling out from a headscarf that perfectly matched the colour of her lips.

"My name is Shania McNeil. I was brought up by Stan Collins and my mother Gloria at the Great Jones fish and chip shop. I knew from an early age Stan and his brother Carl were dealing in dodgy stuff. Carl wanted me to run errands for him, but my mother Gloria always stood up to him."

Adam frowned. There was a discrepancy here with Stan's statement that needed checking. One more thing, then, to add to an already very long list.

"When I was fifteen, Carl introduced me to Frank Fogarty. He seemed so kind and he made me feel very special. He would buy me designer clothes, take me to fancy restaurants, give me the latest phone. I fell in love almost at once, and we started sleeping together three months before my sixteenth birthday.

"But I soon learnt the hard way there was always a payback with Frank. He said that if I loved him, I had to do stuff for him. I did not want to, but he never gave me a choice. When I learnt that he was going to stand trial for rape, I got scared, real scared. But I did not feel I could tell anyone.

"In the end my mother found out anyway. She was so angry with Stan and blamed him for everything. That's when she left, and moved back to Jamaica. She begged me to go with her and I wanted to, I wanted more than anything to be with her. But Frank said he could have me put away for life. He was the police, and he could plant whatever evidence he liked.

"I stopped seeing Frank just before the trial started. By that time he was 45, I was 17. I knew Frank would be found not guilty, and I knew all I could do was stay and do whatever I was asked to do. That's how I ended up working for Carl and then Lewis. I had no choice."

Patience took off her reading glasses and addressed Adam directly. "It is my contention that my client is a victim rather than a perpetrator of crime."

"That will be for a jury to decide," said Adam. He looked back at Shania across the table and saw she had slumped over, with her head buried in her arms, as if trying to block out what she had just heard. "But what I can say is that your client has been extremely brave, and I will do all I can to bring Frank Fogarty to justice."

"Gloria McNeil is coming over next week to visit her daughter. She has already agreed to provide you with a statement supporting Shania's allegations."

"I will be on leave from the Friday," said Adam. Come hell or high water, he was going to spend a week with Sadie, no matter what new material came his way. That date in his calendar was his light on the horizon, however faint at times it had shone recently.

"She'll be here before then," smiled Patience, "and my client is aware you, or another officer, may wish to speak with her again."

Adam nodded. He would have to speak to DI Spencer, of course, but at least this part of the case could be handed over to a specialist team, and he needed all their expertise when it came to the sexual assault of a minor.

"Thank you for all you have shared," said Adam, opening his briefcase. "But before I go, I have to ask – is your client willing to describe any of the errands she carried out?"

"That is something my client is not willing to disclose at this stage."

Adam understood the answer perfectly. Maybe later, then, as the investigation progressed. He would bear that in mind.

"One final question. Can you provide any information at all about the death of Niall O'connor?"

Patience and Shania conferred. "Off the record, a name. Mason Clarke."

Adam frowned. There were so many names in this case it was hard to remember them all. He thought hard and realised this was the lad who had attacked the police van with a scaffolding pole. He was due in court next week. Maybe if the ever faithful DC Sawyer was free, he might be able to follow up that lead in time.

By now it was lunchtime and Adam was hungry. As he left to look for somewhere nearby to eat, he couldn't help thinking about Frank Fogarty. He had recently started saying the Lord's Prayer, and the more the case developed, the more the phrase "deliver us from evil" resonated with him. Frank thought nothing of seducing women, or indeed girls, to further his schemes, was happy to traffic children, and cared nothing for the misery his business inflicted on others. But where was he? So far every search had been fruitless, both in this country and abroad. Yet he vowed he would keep on looking, and he dreamt that maybe, just maybe he might be the one to arrest him. That would be a sweet moment indeed.

Meanwhile, just as Adam was dropping into a local bakery, DI Gregory was finishing a meeting to review the case so far against Billy Hurst. A murder thirty years ago in a remote location always produced few leads, and progress was painfully slow in this case. Partial DNA profiles had been retrieved from the Ford Granada that matched to Billy Hurst and Timmy Taylor but was there enough evidence to bring a conviction? That was the question the team had been exploring that morning and there was a feeling of gloom that perfectly matched the weather outside.

DI Gregory glanced at his phone to see if it was time for a break, frustrated by the lack of progress. It was then he noticed there were two voicemails waiting for him from an unknown number.

Suspiciously he pressed play and then swore as he listened to Jo Pennycome's messages.

DI Gregory was generally not a man given to swearing, which is why his sudden outburst of expletives shocked everyone present.

"Something the matter?" asked the soon to be retired DS Stoneycliffe.

"Adam's sister has discovered a suitcase buried in the trees just behind Little Netherworthy Lodge."

"The trees we couldn't investigate because we had used up our budget?"

"Yes, those trees we couldn't investigate because we had used up our budget. Now the higher ups will be demanding why we didn't look there."

"There's a reason why I'm getting out of here."

"Pity us poor sods who have to stay," said DI Gregory bitterly. "Right then, let's get the ball rolling, and I'll ring Jo back."

In the fading light of an already bleak and unkid afternoon, the crime scene investigation team with their white protective suits descended once again on Little Netherworthy. Jo watched as they erected a tent and set up floodlights. She had a deadline to meet on a chemical patent, but the discovery of that morning had destroyed her concentration. Suddenly that sense of solitude she had enjoyed so far felt menacing, and she wasn't so sure she wanted to be alone. But she had nowhere else to go, and no means of transport. There was just time to go up the road and get a couple of bottles. Maybe by morning the sense of calm would return. Certainly she reasoned, she would have no memory of the night.

Chapter 21

ADAM ONLY LEARNT OF THE contents of the suitcase when the trial began on that wet miserable day the following November. All he knew at the time was that Jo's discovery had for some unspecified reason led to the arrest of Billy Hurst. That news at least provided him with some cheer at the end of a particularly depressing afternoon.

He had been attending the funeral of Tommy Taylor; few others had been present and in the bleakness of the cold, decrepit crematorium Timmy's parents, Eric and Dawn, wept in near total isolation. The service, such as it was, had been led by a civil celebrant who was clearly practised in the art of fake compassion, particularly when she read a poem about death being nothing at all. It was a relief afterwards to get outside into the warmth and honesty of a late autumn sunset, where the few floral tributes provided just the merest hint of life.

"Thank you for coming," said Dawn, her eyes still red from weeping.

"Took you long enough to find our Timmy, didn't it?" added Eric bitterly.

"Not now, love," said Dawn, touching his arm.

"Not that I blame you personally, you understand. Just keep catching the bastards, that's all."

Adam smiled. That was the exact phrase Uncle David had used when he had last seen him. Was that really less than a year ago? So much had happened since then, and he suddenly realised just how much he needed clarity about the future.

Thirty-six hours until he was with Sadie. But first there was just one thing he needed to do.

Adam set out for Newcastle-upon-Tyne in Uncle David's faithful old Micra just as soon as the rush hour had passed. He had all day to get there, and he didn't really mind his relatively slow and sedate progress. He had left the ongoing and increasingly complex investigation in as much order as possible, and he knew DC Stuart Sawyer would do as professional and thorough a job as possible in his absence. So as the motorway stretched ahead, he was aware of his heavy burden starting to lift, and a possibly unwarranted sense of optimism began to brighten his mood.

Surely and steadily, then, the miles began to fall away. Soon enough, he was travelling through the East Midlands, and Adam, aware it was time for lunch, decided on a whim to turn off in search of Broadleigh Manor Hotel. It was relatively easy to find, a relic of a bygone age surrounded by squat bungalows and terraces of narrow two up, two downs. As Adam approached, he drove down a rough, potholed driveway, all the time wondering what it must have been like for Sadie to grow up there. He hadn't really thought what he might do if he bumped into her parents, or if they recognised him, but somehow he felt it would be all right.

As it turned out, there was no awkward encounter. He ate a surprisingly tasty lunch of chicken pie and chips, followed by strawberry cheesecake, surrounded by sales reps who all seemed to be either wrapping up deals on their mobiles, or entertaining reluctant clients on their expense accounts. Even off duty, he couldn't help suspecting at least some of them of dodgy business, but he knew it was not his place to judge.

He needed to stretch his legs before folding his frame back into the little hatchback. As he wandered around the hotel grounds he noticed the faded decor and the cracked paving. Sadie had mentioned something about her parents possibly retiring. Certainly, the whole site would need substantial investment, and soon.

He arrived in Newcastle on a cold, frosty evening. He had found a budget hotel close to a gym where he could spend a couple of hours working out before a fitful night's sleep. Then he headed off early to another crematorium, this time to attend the funeral of Niall O'connor.

The contrast in the two services could not be greater. This one was led by a very elderly Roman Catholic priest who remembered Niall as a tousled headed boy who would run away from home and hide in the church. There was a warmth in his recollections, and a genuine sadness in what had happened since. Adam did not understand the meaning of all the rituals, but it seemed to him there was at heart a genuine hope that the scattered mourners needed.

"I'm surprised to see you here," said Maire, Niall's sister.

"Thought it was the least I could do. I wish we'd found out some other way, but Niall's death led us to smash a major drugs' ring."

"There'll be another one to take its place, soon enough."

"Of that I am certain."

Maire inhaled from her vape and looked at Adam directly with her sad, haunted eyes. "I always knew this day would come, ever since I first introduced him to heroin."

"But you can't blame yourself."

"Oh, I can. Niall and me, we had a shit childhood. I escaped by finding drugs and boyfriends who pretended to care for me. Then I let one start slipping stuff to Niall. He was only fourteen – may the saints forgive me."

"Yet somehow you got clean."

"Aye. I was nineteen, and I decided I wanted to keep me babby. It was hell being pregnant and trying to kick the drugs. Motherhood was even worse. Somehow I managed it, even got an education. I only wish to God I could have saved Niall."

"You found him. You called him. He knew he wasn't alone any more."

"Still doesn't make me feel better."

"You better go now, you're only upsetting her." A painfully thin lad in a cheap creased suit came up and hugged his mother protectively.

Maire offered a bony handshake, which Adam accepted, and then he was on his way.

As Adam approached Sadie's place of work, he found himself more and more confused by the instructions on his Satnav. The postcode was right, but the location was wrong, and finding his way to the right industrial unit was a matter of educated guesswork. Eventually he pulled up at the very end of a service lane where a small, neat sign advertised her business. He paused for a moment, uttered a silent prayer and then made his way towards the narrow steel door.

Sadie was wearing denim dungarees and a white long-sleeved top underneath, with her thick auburn hair tucked neatly into a bun, and disposable gloves on her hands. She was surrounded by cardboard boxes, with her laptop open in front of her, and it was clear she was in the midst of the Christmas rush.

Nonetheless, when she heard the door open, she looked up with that same warm, open smile Adam found entrancing, took off her gloves and gave him a long embrace.

"Do you need lunch? There's a flask of soup and some fresh bread in the back office. Sorry I can't stop, I have thirty-four orders to fulfil before 5pm."

"No worry, it's just good to see you."

"And I you. There's tea and coffee and flapjack as well."

Adam lightly kissed Sadie on the cheek and then went into the office. He was just finishing lunch and about to put the kettle on when he heard the door open.

"Tucker! How the hell did you find me?" asked Sadie, clearly startled.

"My old friend Damian. Did he never tell you? We were at school together. He was the one who told me to look out for you when you first came to Oz."

"I told you," said Sadie, her voice rising, "I never wanted to see you again."

"But I was visiting Damian and I thought, why not drop by?"

Adam had heard enough. He got up, strode into the unit to see Sadie visibly shaking and in the entrance a confident, relaxed ginger dude with his arms crossed, and a rather unpleasant grin.

"Is there a problem?" asked Adam, using a phrase employed many times before when, as so often, he was the first at the scene of an incident.

"And who are you?" asked Tucker.

"Although I am off duty, I am for the purposes of this conversation, DS Adam Pennycome."

"Ah, yes, the famous secret lover. I have read all about you."

Sadie moved closer to Adam. "I used to fear you," she said quietly, "but not anymore."

"You English have a phrase, what is it? A knight in shining armour. How sweet."

Adam had had enough. "I am going to ask you to leave now."

"And what if I don't?" asked Tucker, moving forward.

Sadie never forgot how with surprising agility Adam came towards

Tucker, dodged a punch, and swept his legs out from under him. He pinned Tucker on his back, and held his hands in a half-nelson.

"Now, do you want my colleagues to put you in handcuffs, or will you get out of my sight, and stay out of Sadie's way?" Adam pressed his knee down hard at this point.

Adam frogmarched Tucker into the car park, where Tucker's hire car was standing. "I now have your registration plate, and your description. We'll be keeping a close eye on you."

Not until Tucker had driven away did Adam turn round and head back indoors. Sadie was still standing in the same spot, the colour drained from her face, her hands down by her sides clenched into a painfully tight ball.

"Tucker tried to rape me," she said in a flat, expressionless tone. "Then he stalked me."

Adam advanced towards her, but she shook her head.

"Lock the door and I will tell you the whole story."

They went into the back office where Adam made coffee with plenty of sugar. There was one comfortable chair where Sadie sat, while Adam found himself squeezed behind a desk full of neatly filed paperwork.

"I told you about Damian, my ex. I didn't know about him and Tucker but now I know why Tucker sought me out. I just thought he was fascinated by an English girl who could play cricket. So he started inviting me out to stuff, and when I said no, he got pretty persistent. But then men are like that sometimes, aren't they? And I somehow convinced myself he was harmless."

Here Sadie's voice faltered a little, and she took a long, slow slurp of coffee as she regained her composure.

"Take your time," said Adam behind the desk, aware he was slipping into professional interviewing mode.

"So one day after nets, I went back to Tucker's flat with a couple he had introduced me to. It all seemed harmless enough, we had a couple of bevvies – nothing more. Then the couple get a call from the babysitter, make their excuses and go. I stand up and I say I really ought to go too. And that's when Tucker makes his move on me."

"Can I ask what happened?"

"As he forced himself on me, I reached for anything, anything at all, that might be at hand. I found my fingers gripping a cricket ball just as he pinned me against the wall. I smashed it as hard as possible into the side of his face, and as he momentarily lost his grasp, I bolted for the door. That's how I escaped, though I am not sure how."

"What happened next?" asked Adam, rather wishing he had ground Tucker's head into the floor.

"I reached the ground floor, threw up and then, as I looked in my bag for a hankie, realised I had left my keys and phone behind. That's when I knew I was in big trouble. I made my way to my friend Grace, and her mother let me stay above the restaurant until the locks were changed at my flat. Even then, I was scared to return, and I would often see Tucker parked outside. That's when Grace and Ruby decided I was never going to be left alone. Whoever was off duty slept at my place, or invited me back to theirs."

"Why didn't you go to the police?"

Sadie uttered a hollow laugh. "Adam, except for Tucker, the Magee family are the police. Dad, sister, brother, probably uncle, auntie, grandad. What was I supposed to do? I knew I simply had to survive. I didn't contact you because I was sure Tucker was reading anything I posted. And I wanted to keep you out of this."

Adam looked at Sadie and she smiled a weak, weary smile. Now he understood why she hadn't kept in touch, now he knew why she had kept him at a distance.

"But if I don't crack on, I am going to have a lot of unhappy customers. Care to lend a hand?"

That night Adam struggled to sleep. They had arrived home at about six and after a quick meal they had settled down to watch some American legal drama they were both moderately interested in. But Sadie was falling asleep by the end. She gave him a gentle kiss and then she slipped off to bed on her own. And Adam knew he was tired too; the long, gruelling weeks of investigation had mentally fatigued him, and he was in need of a break. However, even as he lay down on her sofa, that deep, refreshing sleep he needed eluded him. He was playing through all that Sadie had shared, and trying to weigh what these revelations might mean for their relationship. But he could reach no firm conclusions. So he thought and he prayed and then he dozed. Then he woke, and he thought and prayed some more until once again he dozed. And so the process went on and on through the long weary hours of the night, an interminable loop of uncertainties and possibilities from which there seemed no obvious escape.

Adam needed to go for a run. It was still only six in the morning, and pitch black outside, as he stepped out onto the frosty street where the very first risers were already scraping their windscreens. He wasn't sure of his route, but he found his way out of the estate of low squat maisonettes, down through a genteel estate of semi-detached bungalows to a canal towpath. The signboard was covered in graffiti, yet Adam suddenly realised this canal led directly to the place where Sadie had first mentioned going to Melbourne, just after they had first slept together. It was of course too far for Adam to run there that morning, but he could choose to go in that direction. So he pounded the path with his measured, rhythmical gait, until it became suddenly clear what he needed to do, and then he turned round and went back the way he had come.

Adam showered, got dressed and went into the kitchen area to make breakfast. He put on the coffee machine, found some oats and some milk and made porridge. Then he looked in the fridge and found some eggs which he scrambled while he toasted the end of a spelt loaf.

Eventually Sadie emerged, wrapped in a pastel coloured floral dressing gown, with the sleep still heavy on her eyes. "Something smells fantastic. That must be why I woke up hungry."

"I believe in a proper start to the day. By the way, do you have any maple syrup?"

"It's in this cupboard," explained Sadie. As she brushed past him he could feel the gentle touch of her hand upon his shoulder and the warmth of her body. But he didn't feel he could reach out and reciprocate the contact – at least, not yet.

They sat down for breakfast, with Adam on the sofa and Sadie nestled into the comfy chair opposite, with a low coffee table between them. They chatted for a while about food, about the weather, about church that morning and Adam's first meeting with her parents. Then the conversation paused, and Adam became very aware of the low hum of the refrigerator and the steady tick of the clock on the wall.

"So," said Adam, unusually slowly, "I have been thinking a lot about all you shared with me yesterday."

Sadie looked at him directly, her eyes now wide awake and attentive. Part of her very much feared what he was going to say next.

"When you came back from Australia, I assumed we would start to sleep together, then maybe live together and then decide whether we wanted to commit to each other. That's usually how it works nowadays, isn't it?"

"I guess."

"But I now see you wanted to know if you could trust me."

"I also had to ask if I was prepared to trust anyone again." Sadie nervously brushed her tousled hair behind her ears.

"A few weeks ago I heard a sermon on the theme of covenant. I didn't understand it fully – but the vicar kept using the phrase 'unconditional commitment'. That led me to think about you and me, about us. So it seems to me the usual order of things is wrong. The commitment has to come first, before anything else."

"So what exactly are you saying?"

At that point Sadie saw for a first time a certain softness and vulnerability in Adam's chiselled features, and a tender expression she had never noticed before.

"I am saying I am seriously thinking of going out and buying a ring to show just how committed I am to you."

That was not at all what Sadie had expected to hear, but she felt her heart leap at what he was saying. "You know – actually you don't know – I have spent many hours recently trying to work out our future. My business here, your life in London, Little Netherworthy Lodge, they're all parts of a complicated jigsaw I haven't been able to fit together. Not, that is, until just now."

"So is that a yes?"

Sadie leant awkwardly across the table and kissed Adam on the lips. "What do you think?"

Adam wanted to take her in his arms, but, as Sadie pointed out, the future Mr and Mrs Pennycome needed to get to church, and she wasn't dressed yet.

The church of Holy Trinity was a barn that on a cold December morning refused to become much warmer than the air outside, but the people who greeted the couple walking in, hand in gloved hand, were friendly and helpful. Adam could follow the words because he had said them at St Alban's, Little Netherworthy, and no-one minded his gruff attempts to sing the first hymn.

Then everyone sat down for what Adam now knew was called the prayer of preparation. As they did so, with much rustling of papers and not a few hearty coughs, the elderly, white-haired vicar simply invited everyone to read the prayer for themselves before they said it out loud together. So Adam began to read: "Almighty God, to whom all hearts are open, all desires known, and from whom no secrets are hidden…"

So many secrets had come to light over the past few months. He thought of Eric and Dawn Taylor sitting down to Sunday lunch, just the two of them, without the extra place setting they had always put out for so many years. He thought of Maire O'connor scattering her brother's ashes in a bleak and desolate garden of remembrance. He thought of Lewis Sinclair and his mother Carol, of Shania McNeil and Frank Fogarty, who despite intensive enquiries at home and abroad remained at large, and he tried not to think what other secrets might be lying buried within the Great Jones fish and chip shop.

Then there was Great Uncle David. Did he deliberately leave the letters behind so Adam could find the woman he had loved? And were there others? Those were questions Adam knew he could never resolve. And what about the Ford Granada estate? Had David had his suspicions about his tenant and the patio? Only Almighty God really knew, and hard as it might be, he had to leave the matter in His hands.

By now the time of confession was over, and Sadie had stood up for the next hymn. She glanced down at him, and he automatically stood up, although he had no idea what he was supposed to sing. Sadie too had borne a heavy secret, and he loved her all the more now, in spite of her reservations, she had put her trust in him. He only hoped he would prove himself worthy of that trust in all the years that were still to come.

All this and more Adam tried to explain to Sadie on the way home. "We best include this prayer in our wedding, then, hadn't we?" she said as she turned into her parking space.

Outside the front door was a garish bouquet of roses and chrysanthemums, with a simple message from Damian: "I am so sorry."

"What do you want to do with them?" asked Adam.

"My mum would think they were lovely. I tell you what, let's take the card off and you can give them to your future mother-in-law."

"I would be delighted," said Adam, and in that moment both were as one in a sense of pure and utter joy.

Printed in Great Britain
by Amazon

41783542R00108